KISSING
EMMA

SHAPARAK KHORSANDI

ORION CHILDREN'S BOOKS

First published in Great Britain in 2021 by Hodder and Stoughton

1 3 5 7 9 10 8 6 4 2

Text copyright © Shaparak Khorsandi, 2021

A CIP catalogue record for this book is available from the British Library.

ISBN: 978 1 51010 699 4

Typeset in Goudy Old Style BT by Jouve (UK), Milton Keynes
Printed and bound in Great Britain by Clays Ltd, Elcograf S.p.A.

The paper and board used in this book are from well
managed forests and other responsible sources.

Orion Children's Books
An imprint of
Hachette Children's Group
Part of Hodder and Stoughton
Carmelite House
50 Victoria Embankment
London EC4Y 0DZ

An Hachette UK Company
www.hachette.co.uk
www.hachettechildrens.co.uk

Dedicated to the memory of Nyousha Movagharzadeh,
the most wonderful, adored and talented young woman,
whose excitement was so catching
1/11/1995–30/7/2019

This story touches on some hard-hitting themes. If you find yourself affected by them, there is a list of resources at the end that may be helpful.

ONE

When your mum has been all over the internet, accused of murdering your dad, well, life changes.

We weren't the perfect family. My dad wasn't the sort who would put me up on his shoulders and call me his little princess. He was more the shut-your-mouth-or-I'll-knock-your-teeth-out type.

Not the whole time. He had his moments. Sometimes he took me to the pub with him. I'd only be little, about six, and he'd buy me a lemonade and pour a bit of his beer in it, which made it taste funny. I wouldn't show it on my face, though, because when I drank it, my dad patted my back and said, 'That's my girl!' That little bit of praise from him made me feel so happy. Proud. His mates would all laugh and say, 'Chip off the old block!' I know it doesn't sound like the most fun afternoon, but when I was little, it was one of the few times I had his attention for a *good* reason.

He'd drink and tell his mates stories that made no sense to me, but when they roared and hung on to his every word, he was a king in my eyes. That was my dad. Fun sometimes, then giving my mum a black eye sometimes. All dads were like that, weren't they? That's what I thought, anyway.

I'd see other dads: the ones down the park, laughing with their kids, talking to them, gently taking them off a climbing frame or carrying them on their shoulders. They'd give the mum a little kiss while the kids played. But they couldn't be like that all the time, I'd think. I bet at home they were all like my dad. I bet they were angry and shouted and made the mum cry – but when they were out and about, they were gentle.

I loved my dad. I honestly did. Even when he was off his head, shouting, and the woman in the flat below would bang on her ceiling with her cricket bat. (I reckon she had to stand on her dining room table to do that.) Sometimes he ran out of our place to tell her to 'shut up you mad old bitch', which gave me and Mum a bit of a breather.

We'd know, just from the way he walked into a room or came into the flat, what mood he was in. Just by his footsteps, we knew whether he was going to start on us or not. Mum would say, in a voice so low only I could hear, 'Go to your room, Emma.' Low and urgent. I would flee, no eye contact with Dad, and go straight to my room. I'd look nowhere but straight ahead, my legs moving despite feeling numb with fear. I'd get under my bed and curl up as tight as I could, putting my hands over my ears to block out whatever noise my mum and dad were making. Shouts, cries, Mum begging. That was the worst. I'd wait for the air to go still, and then Mum would come and crouch by my bed, reaching her hand underneath it for me to hold. I'd take it and crawl out, without looking at her. It always seemed too soon to look. Instead I'd just press against her, and she would hold me. When it was safe, Mum would sort out whatever mess he had made of the flat and of her.

As I got older, there were more bad bits than good bits. Dad's stories and jokes all got swallowed up by a stream of ranting and swearing. He drank at home, then he went out and drank again. He picked on Mum even more. She was 'fat' and a 'hag'. Whatever she made for him to eat was 'a plate of shite'. Then he'd turn to me, saying I was just as big a waste of space, that I was always in his way. Eventually he'd storm out of the flat, shouting and swearing as he went. I'd hear him all the way down the stairwell, calling me and Mum names that drifted back up to us. When he came back, we never mentioned whatever row had gone on before.

For some reason, I never learned my lesson. Every time he came back and wasn't shouting, I would think that was it. Maybe it would never happen again. Maybe that was the last time he'd ever start on us. I thought that every single time. I'd be good. I'd be so good he'd never shout at me again.

But there was just no way of knowing. Sometimes he said to Mum, 'Put some slap on, you look half-dead,' so she'd do her face. But if she put on some lipstick and a bit of mascara without him telling her to, he'd scream, 'You look like a tart!' till she cried and took it off. No way of predicting it.

Really, the only good bits when I was little were when it was just me and Mum. 'You are not an only child,' Mum used to say to me. 'You're the *one and* only child!'

When Dad wasn't around, Mum was different. She was fun. 'Wanna dress up in my clothes, Emma?' I'd put on one of her dresses, wear her shoes and she'd put make-up on me. 'Go on. Do one of your impressions!' she'd say. I could really make her laugh. With bright pink lipstick and a pen in my mouth for a cigarette, I'd be Dora, the woman who lived above us and was constantly smoking on her balcony. Those cigarettes were always blowing on to ours after she'd flicked them out. I called her Mrs And-Why-Shouldn't-I?, because that's what she always said.

'Me husband' – I did her voice raspy and deep – *'says I smoke too much. And why shouldn't I? It's not 'is business. I don't moan that he farts so much I can't light a match in the house, do I? I like to sit on the balcony in the fresh air and shout at the kids down there playing. And why shouldn't I? I drive Mary downstairs mad with my shouting and my fag ends – and why shouldn't I?'*

Mum would laugh and laugh, telling me, 'I honestly wouldn't know the difference with my eyes shut, Emma! You got a gift! But keep it down, she'll hear you.'

Mum didn't like me playing on the estate with the other kids after school. 'You're a cut above, my darling,' she'd tell me. 'You've got *prospects*. You're intelligent, you're beautiful. I'm not saying there's anything wrong with them kids out there . . .'

I'd roll my eyes and smile. 'But you are, Mum.'

'I'm not. I just don't think they're going anywhere. This estate sucks you in if you let it, and I won't let that happen to you.'

I didn't mind not going out to play. I had Mum to do things with. We'd watch all the soaps together, and I'd do impressions of the actors. She'd get these magazines full of all the celebrities and we'd guess who'd had their lips done, who'd had their boobs done. I stared at these girls on the glossy pages, and the lives they led, all shiny hair and rich boyfriends. They holidayed on yachts and sparkled at parties. It was another world, but these were the sort of places Mum thought I could go one day. She said I was pretty enough, and sometimes I'd think that maybe she was right. But back then, Mum and I just got lost in dreaming.

*

'What do you want more bloody books for?' my dad moaned when Mum and I brought a couple back from the charity shop one day. 'You already got a whole load of 'em, taking up all the room in here!' He said it like we'd gone out and bought saucepans when we already had a perfectly good set in the cupboard.

'But I've read those ones, Dad,' I said carefully.

'You've read all them books?' Dad scoffed. 'Then you're *sad*, my girl. You need to get a life or you'll end up like your mother.' He pointed his beer bottle at Mum, and it sloshed a bit on to the carpet. I got away with it that time, my shoulders sagging in relief.

I kept my books so perfect. Tucked in beside each other, tallest to shortest. Mum called me a book worm. It made me smile to think of being a worm, burrowing into my books to escape. We'd go to the library sometimes, but there were some books I loved so much I liked to read them again and again, and you always had to give library books back. I liked having my own to keep.

Mum read me *The Secret Garden* at bedtimes. It was one of my favourites. I'd imagine there was a secret garden on our estate, behind the high grey wall at the end. There wasn't, of course. It was a samosa factory, but I'd still pretend. I had my books and a few toys in my little room that Mum painted pink for me.

When I was six, my absolute favourite toy was Speaking

Baby. She had shiny, dark hair like mine, and you pressed her hand and she went, 'Ma-ma.' She wasn't just a doll to me. She was real. She had feelings and she loved me. When my mum and dad were fighting and I was off under my bed, I'd take her with me, holding her close to me, protecting her. 'It's OK, Speaking Baby, I'll look after you,' I'd whisper to her. Every moment when I wasn't at school, I played with her. Rocking her to sleep in my arms, I sang her lullabies. I kissed her and tucked her in beside me in bed every night. I knew she could hear me. When I was sad or scared, I cuddled her close and she understood how I was feeling.

Sheila upstairs had given me Speaking Baby for my sixth birthday. She worked at the big supermarket, the one you had to get the bus to. She said to my mum, 'It weren't dear. I got my staff discount. I saw it in the shop and couldn't resist.'

Sheila lived with Mike. They were older than my mum and dad and didn't have kids. I was too small, then, to know you didn't just blurt out, 'Why haven't you got children?' at people.

'God didn't bless us with children, my darling,' Sheila told me.

For a long time I wondered why God didn't bless Sheila with kids. How could he have looked at lovely, kind Sheila and gone, 'Nope. Not trusting you with a baby,' but then looked at my dad and thought, 'He's fine, he can have one'?

Sheila and Mike's flat was my favourite place to be. It never smelled of fish fingers like ours did. It smelled of baking and Sheila's bowl of lavender potpourri. That bowl of dried woodchips, smelling of garden flowers, was to me the most sophisticated thing anyone could possibly have in their hall. Their flat was exactly the same size and shape as ours, but it looked so different – all plush, with their big, green, soft sofa and proper curtains, not plastic blinds like at ours.

'Can I go upstairs, Mum?' I'd ask almost every afternoon. Mum would nod with a mixture of relief and sadness on her face, then stand at the bottom of the stairs until she heard Sheila greet me with her warm, "Ello, my darling! You wanna come in for some milk and biccies?' Mum would shout up behind me, 'That all right, Sheila? Just send her down when she's a nuisance.'

'You're never a nuisance, are you, my darling?' Sheila would say to me. 'Come in. Mike! We got our little visitor.' Mike would wave at me from his chair and carry on watching TV. Somehow there was always football on.

The day after my sixth birthday, Sheila sat me down at her little table in the kitchen and gave me Speaking Baby. She showed me how I could make it talk by giving it a little squeeze.

'Ma-ma,' the doll said.

'See?' Sheila said. 'You're her mama, and you got to look after her just like your mummy does with you.'

When I was back downstairs that night, I tucked up in bed with my new doll and told her, 'It's OK, baby. Everything will be OK.'

Then one night, more than a whole year after I got Speaking Baby, I heard my dad come in really late. His footsteps thumping into the flat made my heart beat so fast that my chest hurt and it was hard to catch my breath. And the moment he came in, he started a fight with Mum.

'This place is a tip!' he yelled. 'And you're off in the land of Nod? Get out here and sort it!' He must have woken her up specially to have the fight.

The screams and thuds sent me under my covers. I heard Mum say, 'Shut up, you'll wake Emma.' Dad shouted back a fiery reply, but it was muffled at first. Mum was saying, 'Leave her alone!' and then I heard Dad more clearly. 'I'm so sick and fucking tired of you and your fucking brat, sponging off me and making a bloody mess!'

Before I could move under the bed, my bedroom door crashed open and in came my dad, yanking my covers off. Mum ran in after him, holding her bleeding head.

Dad grabbed my arm and pulled me out of bed. He made me stand in front of him and he was bellowing in my face. I couldn't even understand what he was saying. It was a load of swearing and calling me horrible names, and he was shaking me as he shouted. I was crying; I didn't know what I had done wrong. My eyes stung from the alcohol on his breath.

He stumbled backwards a bit, tripping over something. Speaking Baby. But when I moved to pick her up, he stomped his boot down, kicking me out of the way. Then he grabbed my doll, still raging, and took two giant, wobbling steps over to my window. We were on the twelfth floor, but he opened it, holding up my doll by her arm.

'No, Daddy, no!' I begged him, sobbing. 'Please, Daddy!'

He looked at me for a second – then hurled Speaking Baby out into the darkness.

I stared at his empty hands as what he had done sank in. Then I let out a wail that rattled my skull. I didn't care if he got angry. I didn't care what he would do to me. The noise seemed to force him away, though. He stormed out of my room, hissing, 'Shut the fuck up!' but I couldn't. My side was sore from where he'd kicked me, but I didn't care about that either.

Mum could finally come to me and hold me while I sobbed for my doll.

'Can we go down and get her?' I wailed. 'Please, Mummy, can we go and get her?'

But Mum begged me to be quiet. 'Please, darling, we can't, we just can't. Not right now. She'll be OK, don't worry.' Nothing she said helped. All I could picture was my doll lying all alone on the filthy ground where I couldn't get to her. The thought gave me more pain than any of his kicks, punches or shoves ever could.

Mum put me in my bed and stayed with me until I finally got exhausted from crying and fell asleep.

In the morning, it took a second to remember the horror of the previous night. I scrambled out of bed and pressed my face to the window, wincing at the ache in my side. It hurt where he had kicked me. There'd be a bruise I would examine later. For the time being, I just looked desperately down on the ground for my doll, but I couldn't see her.

A big lump had grown beside the cut on Mum's forehead overnight. She held an ice pack to it, and I could tell she was desperate for it to go down before she faced my dad. None of us ever mentioned his rages once they had passed, and having visible injuries from the night before felt like mentioning it. We knew it would make him feel like Mum was taunting him. That's what he'd sometimes say when she limped around, bruised, fetching him breakfast after another rough night. 'Are you taunting me, Mary?'

Dad woke up and lumbered into the bathroom without a word. But Dad being quiet didn't mean safety. I had to be extra careful. I mustn't talk about the doll, even though I really wanted to go and look for her. We'd have to wait until he went out.

When Dad emerged, still belching last night's alcohol, Mum quietly served him his breakfast. She got my toast too, and set it down in front of me. I chewed on a corner, feeling tears building up again, but it was too dangerous to cry.

Dad pushed his plate away. 'I can't take being stuck in this flat with you two miserable bitches moping about,' he hissed, then grabbed his coat and went out of the door.

The minute it shut, my breath came back. The whole flat felt lighter. Mum and I looked at each other, waiting a few minutes to be sure he was gone. Then Mum got a cap and pulled it over her head, wincing as it touched her bruise. She got my coat, put it on me, and we rushed down the stairwell to find Speaking Baby. I insisted on the stairs, because the creaky old lift took for ever and always smelled of piss.

We looked all around the side of the building where Dad had thrown her – under cars, behind the bins, under bushes. Mum said softly that maybe someone had taken her, and my heart burst with hurt. The tears came again in a rush. I hadn't thought of that. What if some other girl had her now? Speaking Baby would never know that I came looking for her. We were too late.

'Please, my darling, stop crying. Stop making all this noise.' Mum was worried about Dad catching us. We couldn't let him see us trying to fix whatever he had broken. We went back inside, and I never saw my beautiful doll again.

TWO

No one saw my dad fall off the balcony. Lots of people heard the row, but no one saw what happened.

I was in my room, in bed, listening to my mum and dad fight. I could hear the whole thing, even with the covers over my head. I was eleven years old by then, a big girl but still scared. I still hid.

My dad was over six foot and heavy. My mum was quite small. Every time they fought, I'd imagine him towering over her. That night, my window was open a crack, so I could hear her screaming on the balcony and him shouting insults back at her.

And then Dad fell.

No one could say they saw Mum do it. But Mum looked guilty because she didn't call the police or ambulance straight away. The people who found his body about ten minutes later were the first to dial 999. All

I heard was yelling, shouting, screaming . . . then suddenly, silence.

Right after, my mum came into my room. Trembling, she held me close and told me, 'Everything is going to be OK.'

The police talked to me again and again.

'I know this is hard for you,' a police officer said gently, 'but I want you to tell me, word for word, what your mum said when she came in to your room that night.'

I was scared talking to the police. What if I said something that got Mum in trouble? I wondered whether I should say, 'My mum said Dad fell by accident.' No. That would be weird. So I told them the truth.

'She said everything was going to be OK.'

'Nothing more?'

'No.' Had I said the wrong thing? Would Mum go to prison?

'Did she call an ambulance before she came into your room?'

'I don't know.'

'Did you see her use her phone? Or hear her?' The police officer spoke to me the way teachers do when you are really little. Softly, so you don't get scared.

'No,' I said. Then, I don't know why, it just came out: 'She screamed,' I blurted.

'Your mum?'

I nodded.

'And Emma, what about your dad? Did you hear him scream or shout?'

'Yes.' My breath was shaky. 'They were fighting.'

'Did you hear him scream or shout when he fell?'

I hadn't. I'd just heard Mum. And then dead quiet. And then she'd come into my room. And that's all I had to tell them.

Mum was with the police for a long time. Even without Dad and his big bear body, all the officers going in and out of our flat made it feel even smaller than it was. They smiled at me, letting me know they were here to help, they were friendly. They looked at the balcony and kept asking questions. They were with my mum so long that Sheila and Mike took me to their house for the rest of the night.

'Blimey, my darling. What a circus,' Sheila said. She closed the curtains and put the TV on for me, making me hot chocolate and giving me biscuits from a batch she'd just baked. Then she sat on the edge of the sofa, which she'd made up into a bed for me, and patted my hand. 'Are you too old for a bedtime story?'

I shook my head. I didn't want her to go. I missed my mum. I didn't want to be alone.

'Well. This is a story from when I was a little girl. My mum read it to me,' Sheila replied, smiling.

She pulled out a book and showed me the cover. It was a story about a girl and her horse. It looked old-fashioned and for a younger kid than me, but I liked hearing Sheila read,

15

sitting on the sofa with my feet under the blanket, resting against her side. I snuggled down, breathed in the lavender scent on the pillow and felt cosy and safe, far away from what was happening in my flat.

The next day, Mum was back – and our estate was on the news. Cameras and presenters, all of that, were stood right outside. Kids went down and made faces behind a reporter's head so they kept having to repeat the same thing again and again down the camera lens. A lot of our other neighbours, even the ones who didn't know us, were talking to the TV people and to the papers.

'Like vultures, they are,' Mike said. 'Vultures feeding off folk's misery.'

I didn't want to watch the news or look online, but I heard Mum FaceTiming Nan from her room.

'So many people have said they heard us fighting.' Mum sounded frightened and was crying.

Nan reassured her. 'People fight all the time, especially husbands and wives, and especially round your way. It don't prove a thing.'

Sheila hardly left our side in those early weeks. She was up and down, baking for us, making my tea when Mum was shut away in her room crying, or on the phone to Nan, or just sitting there, staring into space.

'It's like Mike told you, darling, they can't prove nothing. And he should know, he's been on jury service twice!'

When Sheila thought I was properly engrossed in watching TV, she added to Mum in a low voice, 'We all know what he was like, and frankly no one would blame you if you *did* do it. I'm not judging you either way. I can hear everything anyone says from our hallway. I heard the way he was on at you.'

Suze was Mum's friend from when they were kids. She lived on the other side of the estate and came around a lot more now Dad was gone. Suze had dyed red hair which was up in a ponytail most of the time. She liked to paint her long nails glittery blue, or green, or purple. 'People will believe what they want to believe because they love a bit of drama,' I heard her say. '*Woman snaps and kills husband* is more exciting than *Angry drunk man loses his balance and falls off his balcony.*'

'But *so many* people believe it, Suze!' Mum whispered back, her voice shaky. 'People are calling me a cold-blooded killer!'

'People forget and move on. Do you remember who won *I'm A Celebrity Get Me Out Of Here*? Not this series, but the one before?'

Mum sounded baffled. 'No.'

'Exactly. No one does. At the time though, you were addicted to it.'

'But this ain't a TV show, Suze. This is mine and Emma's life.'

'I know that, my darling, but I'm trying to make you see that people will eventually find something else to chat rubbish about and leave you alone. Believe me.'

Suze knew what she was talking about. Mum had told me that back at school, Suze had had a different name. 'I was always Suze, darling,' she said once when I asked what her old name was. 'Always Suze. It just took a while to tell everyone. Don't matter what they called me when I was born.'

I'd only ever known her as Suze, who lived in Doc Martens boots and vintage dresses and spoke to me like she was interested, never like I was just a little kid. She told me she had been beaten up, spat at, had bottles thrown at her front door. 'Why did you stay living round here?' I asked her.

'Friends, love. Like your mum. This place is my home, where my friends are. Not many of them, mind, but they're all I've got,' she joked.

Mum and Suze would talk for ages while I sat at the kitchen table. 'This won't go away, Suze,' Mum told her. 'This'll never go away.'

Neither, I thought, would the fact that people on our estate knew Suze was trans, but she had survived. Couldn't Mum and I?

Eventually, Mum was officially released without charge, and Dad's death was ruled an accident. Suze was wrong, though. There was no going back to normal for us on the estate. Outside of our four walls, Dad had been the life of the party, a permanent fixture in the local, mates with everyone. Now, when Mum and I passed by, people either looked like they were trying really hard to act normal, or they just narrowed their eyes and stared. Most people stopped talking to us altogether. Even Mrs And-Why-Shouldn't-I? looked away when she saw us. I could just imagine her saying, 'I reckon that Mary's guilty – and why shouldn't I?'

Mum tried not to let it show that it upset her, but I could see it did. She held her head up and would even raise her eyebrow if someone stared at her. She'd just stare back, like she was daring them to say something. They never did.

The estate wasn't the same any more for Mum and me. Not that we'd ever properly been a part of it. Mum hadn't gone drinking down the club with Dad, or with any of the women who made sandwiches for the bar there. We'd always stuck out. It was as if he existed entirely separately to our life on the estate. And now, apart from Suze, and Sheila and Mike upstairs, it was out in the open – no one really liked us.

At Dad's funeral I heard some men, mates of my dad's from down the pub, talking about him. 'The place just won't be the same without him . . .'

'Too right. He was a good man.'

'Solid. Never backed out of a fight.'

Now that was something I knew already.

That day, all these strangers came up to Mum and introduced themselves. She smiled and thanked them for coming, even though something felt off. It was like they wanted to get a closer look at a dangerous animal at the zoo. But somehow, it felt like *we* were the ones in danger.

There was one woman at the funeral who didn't come up to us. She was stood at the back, sobbing so much that people were turning to look.

'Who is that, then?' Nan asked Mum.

Mum said, 'I have no fucking idea.'

It was the first time I'd ever heard my mum swear. It made me think maybe she did know who that woman was. That she felt the general threat in the air, same way I did.

*

Time went on. A year, two years. The crackle of danger around us never really let up. I learned to keep my head down at school. I only really talked to Deana, my best friend. We'd met when, in the first few days of Year Seven, our form teacher made us go around in a circle and tell everyone what we wanted to be when we were older. YouTuber and footballer came up a lot. So did popstar and TV presenter. A few said they wanted to work in a shop. When it got to Deana, sat there in her long skirt and hijab, she smirked and said, 'Nun.' Everyone cracked up.

Deana was funny. I was so proud I was her best friend.

She didn't really bother with anyone else. She didn't care what people thought of her, or if she was popular. 'I should have said "pornstar". Less controversial, innit,' she'd said that first day, after class.

Then we hit Year Nine, and it was time to choose our GCSE subjects.

'I'm not allowed to do Art *and* Drama, Mum. I've got to choose.'

'Well, which are you best at?' Mum asked.

'Dunno.'

Mum said I was more likely to make money doing acting than doing art. 'You could be in a film or on *EastEnders* or something, but no one is going to pay you to draw some fruit in a bowl, are they?'

Our teachers never got tired of telling us how important the next two years were. It was a constant drone.

Deana was taking the whole 'very important' thing much more seriously than I was. 'I wanna go to college,' she said. 'I've got to pass every single GCSE.'

'I wish I could just leave school now and get a job,' I told her.

'A job?' she said, scoffing a bit. 'Like what?'

'I don't know. Any job. Babysitter. Postie. Something like that.'

'Babysitter and postie are very different jobs. You don't want to get muddled up and deliver a baby instead of a letter.'

I gave her a shove, stifling a laugh. I loved her for taking the piss. She made me feel like things were normal. That *I* was normal.

I never told her the truth about why I really wanted a job.

*

A few weeks earlier, someone had painted 'murderer' in red paint over our door. I almost didn't notice it because I was rushing out the door to go to school. The lift came, which I wouldn't usually get, but it was right there so I got in. Just as the lift started to creak shut, I glanced at our front door. There was the big M, and then the rest of the letters were squashed to fit. The letters were like a giant invisible slap, right across my face.

I jumped back out of the lift, forcing my shoulder against the doors to get out.

'What have you forgotten?' Mum said when I raced back into the flat. She had on her tabard and was getting ready to go to work, cleaning one of the big houses on Brunswick Road.

I was crying. 'Mum, look what they've done!' And I pulled her to the door.

Mum stared at it. Her face was upset for a second, but she pushed it away, and then she just looked furious. 'After all this time? Why can't they all just leave us be? Run upstairs and ask Sheila if she's got any white spirit.'

Sheila came downstairs herself with the white spirit and some rags. 'Monsters,' she muttered as she began to scrub.

I wanted to stay and help, but Mum wasn't having it. 'Get to school,' she ordered.

I left them there, both scrubbing, wishing I could get a job, make some money and get us out of this place. The feeling had stuck with me ever since.

Nan had FaceTimed me on the night of the painted door. 'What did you expect? You live in a shithole. Tell your mum you need to come and live with me and your Auntie Jean till she gets back on her feet.'

Back when Dad was around, Nan never used to call or come over. He hadn't liked her, I knew that much. But as soon as he was gone and Auntie Jean had bought Nan a camera phone, she was on FaceTime every day. Often I came home from school and Mum would say, 'Go and have a chat with your nan, she's on the kitchen table.' And there she would be, propped up against the fruit bowl, waiting for me to have a natter.

'Your dad wanted us out of the picture, you know – your mum's family.' It was like Nan had been waiting years to say what she really thought of Dad. 'Your Auntie Jean, I could understand. She gets on the wrong side of *everybody*. But I can't understand why he had a problem with me, Emma, I honestly can't. Just because I had a bit too much to drink at their wedding and shouted out "YOU CAN DO SO MUCH BETTER, MARY" during the ceremony.'

I grinned at the screen. 'You didn't actually, did you, Nan?'

'Best believe I thought it! And there are some thoughts you can't hide from people. They're literally written all over your face, and I reckon he saw them clear as day.'

Nan's idea about us moving in with her and Auntie Jean sounded better and better. It'd be a way out of our problems on the estate.

'Why don't we go live with Nan and Auntie Jean?' I asked. They lived on the other side of London. Three buses away – miles from all the bad memories here.

Mum let out a scoff as she folded up the washing. 'Not sure your Auntie Jean and me could live together for very long,' she said. 'I don't want to be accused of another murder.'

'What about just for a bit, see how it goes?' Apart from Deana, Sheila upstairs and Suze, there was nothing and no one around here I would miss. But my mum wasn't having it.

'Your Auntie Jean reckons I've got airs and graces.'

'If I had a sister, I'd want to live with her,' I said, already feeling a sulk coming on.

'Not if your sister was Jean, you wouldn't. She scrounges off your nan, that's literally all she does.'

'She bought Nan an iPhone though, that's not sponging.'

'*Did* she buy it though? And who off? Believe me, your Auntie Jean won't have the receipt for that phone.'

Auntie Jean's two girls, Becca and Jade, were older than me, eighteen and nineteen. 'Those two would be a bad influence and all. She lets them run wild,' Mum said, 'and they've got no plans to move out of your nan's. If nothing else, there'd hardly be room . . .'

At least they had the chance to run wild. I never did. You couldn't be on our estate at night unless you wanted to risk real trouble – especially after what happened with Dad. Even people who tried to do some good got driven away. A woman tried to set up a youth centre here once. Someone set fire to it in the night. She never came back. That's just how it was round here – and for the time being, I couldn't see a way out.

THREE

Since I made sure I kept my head down, I hadn't ever really had much trouble at school. But there had been whispers, especially from some of the girls from the estate. One day, Keira, Clara and Lainy, the girls everyone pretended to be friends with because they were scared of them, cornered me in the changing rooms after PE.

'My mum saw yours in the gazette the other day. Someone wrote *Murderer* on your door, didn't they?'

I hadn't known it was in the paper. It had taken so long to get off the door, and you could still see the letters faintly even after all Mum and Sheila's scrubbing. Mum never told me any reporters had been sniffing around again.

'So?' I answered, trying to shrug it off. Mostly these girls left me alone. But for whatever reason, today was my turn.

'You're lucky to be alive, you know,' said Keira. 'My mum reckons you should've been taken into care, in case you're the next one to go flying out the window.'

Keira and Clara laughed loudly, clutching each other like that was the funniest thing in the world. The few kids that were left in the changing room hurriedly got their stuff together and fled. If they were going to start on me, no one wanted to get involved.

'Rise above,' Mum always told me. I was going to rise above. My cheeks burned though.

'It wasn't a window,' I murmured.

'What? Oh my God!'

'Did she just say—'

'You should be out of here by now, girls.' Miss Barfoot, the PE teacher, bustled in.

'We were just seeing if Emma was OK, miss,' said Keira.

I was still blinking back tears and fuming. Those girls couldn't have cared less if I was OK or not.

Miss Barfoot looked at me. 'Either way, you need to get yourselves some lunch before the bell goes.'

The girls walked beside me, crowding around me as we walked. 'Did your mum do it, though?' Lainy asked.

I gritted my teeth. 'No.'

'That's not what *my* mum thinks,' Lainy said.

'It's what the police think.'

Lainy smirked. 'Actually, *not enough evidence* just means they can't prove it. Your mum's a murderer.'

Mum had told me to ignore this stuff, but she didn't have to go to school with Lainy Robertson. In a second, my fist had flown out and I'd twisted her jumper in a bunch around her neck, shoving her against the wall. Keira and Clara were so shocked they just stared.

'You don't say that about my mum, OK?' I hissed in Lainy's face. My eyes drilled into her for a few seconds more, then I let her go, turned and left.

She didn't come for me. She looked scared.

I am my father's daughter, after all.

*

'You're the only person in this whole school that doesn't judge me,' I told Deana as we walked through the park after school that day.

'I do judge you,' she replied, 'but only behind your back because that's what *real* friends do.'

Most people didn't know that Deana was funny. I think it's because she wore a hijab. They assumed she'd be dead serious and that they couldn't be themselves with her, but it was their loss. Deana was a laugh.

'People dying is normal in my family,' she told me, a bit more serious now. Deana's family were Iraqi, and it sounded like there were a lot more unexpected deaths in their family

28

than most people's. 'And not just because of war and stuff. I had an aunt that I swear died of embarrassment. This other family had come over to see if she was suitable to marry their son. She was only twenty. The meetings are so formal, really formal – like, if you smile too much, you're a slut, and if you laugh out loud, you're a whore, so—'

'What if,' I interrupted, 'you don't laugh or smile, you just give a cheeky wink?'

Deana kept a dead straight face. 'Wash your mouth out, Emma. No woman in my family has *ever* winked at a man she has not been married to for at *least* thirty years. Anyway, so my aunt, yeah? She served the guy's parents tea, and as she bent down with the tray, she farted! Seriously! It was so bad she just died straight away from the shock! You have no idea how taboo letting one off is in my culture.'

'Not just *your* culture.' I laughed, then I stopped. 'Hey, do you think it was actually suicide? Because she didn't want to marry him?'

Deana clutched my arm dramatically. 'Oh my days, I never thought of it like that! My auntie killed herself! Death by fart!'

We laughed so much that we cried.

Apart from dying of farts, Deana had family who'd died after getting caught up in the war. 'Seriously, my nan's house was bombed twice. She died both times.'

'Ah, Deana!' I couldn't laugh at that. 'Only you could joke about something so dark!'

'If you can't laugh, how can you cope, innit?'

The stuff she said was true. Her dad had half a leg and an eye missing. Deana was British now, but when they first came over they were refugees.

'I didn't even speak English when we arrived,' she told me once. 'I couldn't believe it was a real language, I thought you lot just made it up as you went along. Sometimes I still think you do.'

'Bazooka,' I replied, nodding seriously. 'Bazooka mardy sausage sandwich.'

She cracked up.

I think Deana always liked to take her time on our walks home because her dad was strict. Really strict. Like, maybe not quite like mine had been, but I don't think being at home was exactly relaxing. On non-uniform day, her dad made her wear her school uniform because he thought it was disrespectful not to. She stuffed her other clothes in her bag and changed when she got to school, then changed back before she went home.

'Why is he like that?' I asked her.

She shrugged. 'Dunno. If I say one thing, one word out of line, even slightly; a miniscule bit of cheekiness and—' She made a cutting gesture with her hand across her neck. 'My dad's just mad.'

'Mine was, too. At least yours is still about.'

'Do you miss your dad?'

'Of course I miss him,' I said, sort of robotically. 'Although I didn't see him all that much,' I added quickly, trying to give her a reason why I wasn't crying about him being gone. It was like I was embarrassed by the truth about how he had treated us. 'He was out most of the time.'

'Yeah, but he was still your dad, innit. My dad drives me mad sometimes. He thinks I'll get pregnant if I even look at a guy – but I don't know, man. If I lost him, I'd cry for like ten years.'

'Pregnant? We're thirteen!'

'I know,' she said, rolling her eyes.

You're supposed to miss your parents when they die. I know that. But the truth was, I didn't miss *him*. I missed not having a dad. He was a part of me, so when he died, there was a part of me that went too. I don't think it was a bad part, necessarily.

I didn't tell Deana that sometimes I felt relieved Dad was gone. Not glad he was dead, just relieved every time I'd remember how he used to shout at us, grab us, hit us. That we didn't have to live with how scared he made me and Mum any more.

There are hardly any pictures of me and him when I was a baby. 'He wasn't a fan of pictures,' Mum told me. He wasn't a fan of babies either. He just wasn't a dad the way Deana's dad was. Deana's dad was strict, yeah, but far as I could tell, he would do anything for her. And she had loads of pictures of them together.

Years ago, when Dad was still alive, I remember Suze saying to my mum, 'You know he's got other women, don't you, Mary? Everyone knows.'

It reminded me that my mum and dad were meant to be a couple. But thinking of them romantically together was weird. I didn't think Mum would care if Dad had 'other women'.

'I'm not stupid, Suze. I know what he is,' Mum had told her.

I wondered if Mum had any good memories of Dad at all. So after leaving Deana that day, I asked her.

She stopped washing up. 'What sort of question is that?'

I shrugged. 'Just wanna know.'

There was a pause, like she was about to say something, but she didn't.

'You must miss him a bit?' I prompted. 'There must've been something you liked about him to marry him?'

I held my breath. She might get upset, or snap at me to leave it, or go cold and change the subject.

Mum didn't do any of those things. She went quiet for a minute and I just waited.

Then she said, 'He was different, your dad, when we met. He adored me. He couldn't keep away from me. I was flattered. I ignored warnings, like his temper, like him being so possessive. After you came along, he really changed. Started to act like he hated me.'

I swallowed hard. 'Blimey, Mum, was it my fault?'

'Oh, don't be silly,' she said quickly. 'It was bad already, but having a baby properly ties you to a person, and that's when he couldn't handle it. The responsibility and all my attention being on you. So, no, Emma, I don't miss him.'

It's not what I wanted to hear. I think I wanted to cling to the idea that in some small way we'd been a proper family. 'Not even a tiny bit?'

Now Mum snapped. 'What do you want me to miss, Emma? His fists? His shouting? His other women? Do you want me to miss my purse being empty because he's stolen my food shopping money to piss up the wall? Do you want me to miss sitting here with you, terrified what state he'll be in when he gets home, wondering how I would protect us? No, Emma. I'll go to hell for saying this but I'm glad he's gone. Not glad he's dead, just glad he's gone.'

I was quiet after that.

Dad had worked for a roofing company when I was a baby. Still did from time to time when I was growing up. Mum said he always ended getting sacked. 'Because being drunk on a roof is against health and safety, would you believe?'

'There are other jobs in the world, you know,' I remember Mum saying to him once when I was a bit older. She could tell him what she thought sometimes, if he wasn't drunk and if he was calm. Sometimes he let her say what she wanted, and he'd be OK. He would even listen and agree. The danger was later. He'd turn over what Mum had said, obsess over it. Then suddenly – days, even weeks afterwards – he'd have Mum pressed up against a wall by her throat, hissing, 'Were you calling me lazy? Is that what you were doing?'

I wished I had just a handful of nicer memories of him. I just wanted something to feel normal, like it did for other girls around me. As it was, all I really had was a dead dad – and a whole bloody estate that hated my mum and me because of it.

FOUR

Eventually, Mum did start listening to Nan about us maybe moving in with her. The attitude we got off people on the estate wouldn't let up, and if something dodgy happened in our area, nine times out of ten it was Elmsworth that was mentioned on the local news. 'The notorious Elmsworth estate', as they always called it, had been home to us my whole life. But Nan was right. It was a shithole.

It was always the same. When the sun went down, the older lads came out, hanging around in the stairwell by the lifts. If we got home after dark, Mum would hold my hand and hurry up the stairs. Sometimes there'd be shouting and swearing from the lads. When I was safely inside, I'd look out of the window and see their lurking shadows in the corner of the estate, doing whatever it was they did, making everyone afraid of going out there.

Mum liked to keep what she called a 'low profile'. That was probably part of why everyone looked at us the way they did. Well, that and the business about Dad. But now that I was older, keeping a 'low profile' wasn't always so easy for me.

The boys that hung out on the estate were looking at me now.

I'm not quite sure when it all changed. It was just like one day I woke up, looked at myself in the bathroom mirror, and I didn't look like a little kid any more. My face was different, my arms and legs were longer. My waist nipped in, like a Coke bottle. And I needed a *bra*.

'Looks like yours are going to be bigger than mine,' Mum had said, right in front of the woman measuring me in the shop.

'Mum!' I protested, crossing my arms over my boobs. It was bad enough I had a strange woman fussing about with them. To take the attention off me a bit, I said to the lady measuring me, 'My mum wants a boob job but she can't afford it.'

'Emma!' Mum said, faking shock.

The bra lady was quite proper and didn't know where to put herself.

'She had a poker up her bum, that one,' Mum said, both of us laughing as we left the shop. I tugged at the straps on my shoulders self-consciously, aware that things were changing.

Soon after that, on every walk to and from school, guys would shout out to us as they drove by. Mostly it was just the usual 'all right, darling' pervy stuff from potbellied white van and taxi drivers, cruising past to get a better look.

'Paedo!' Deana would shout at them.

'Deana, don't! They'll think you're flirting,' I'd joke.

If I was on my own, I just tried to ignore the blokes who shouted and whistled. It was scary sometimes when they proper slowed down in their cars to talk to me, hanging out of their windows like panting dogs. I would just turn up the path into someone's front garden, pretending I lived there and they'd quickly drive off.

Some of the boys in school were just as bad. I had the second biggest boobs in our year. Martha Diamond had the biggest – she was excused from trampolining in PE. Boys were always trying to snap our bra straps. They never looked at my face any more – not that they ever did much before. It got funny, but also boring and predictable. Deana and I joked about putting a sign round my neck, saying, 'My eyes are up here.'

School started getting intense. Since I'd stood up to Lainy and her mates, I'd gone from hanging out quietly with Deana to having quite a few of the more loud, popular girls wanting to hang out with me. The ones that whooped and cackled as they barrelled down the corridors in a big line.

I was nice, polite, I had a laugh with them if they chatted to me. But I had Deana. No way did I want to be all chummy with these girls who'd completely ignored me until I got into a fight. That wasn't me. I didn't want that trouble at school. I just wanted to get through it, and get out of there as soon as I could.

Lainy herself tried to get all matey with me around then. It almost made me laugh.

'You know Carlos likes you?' she said to me one day.

Carlos was the really fit boy in our year. She was right, he did like me. I could tell. It was a weird feeling, but I'd seen him staring at me even more than the other boys.

And then one day, he asked me out.

Deana and I were just hanging out on a bench when I felt Carlos' shadow fall over me.

'Hey, Emma. You wanna come to Iceshack after school?' Iceshack was the place on the corner of the high street, where people from school went if they had money to get these massive ice creams in a glass.

I don't know where I got the confidence from, but I smiled and said, 'A date?'

He blushed, which made me smile even more. 'Maybe,' he said.

Deana was still sat next to me, and for some reason she went, 'She ain't going nowhere with you.'

Carlos said, 'Did I ask you though?'

And Deana went, 'No, but she's my mate and I'm saying she don't wanna go nowhere with you.'

Somehow Deana and Carlos ended up having a row before I even got to say anything else. Deana was shouting at him and shooed him away.

'I'll see you later, Emma, maybe when you've left your guard dog at home, yeah?' he threw over his shoulder.

I was mortified. Finally, I found my voice. 'Deana, *what* was that?

'What?'

'He was asking me, not you!'

'Yeah and I was helping you out.'

I felt my jaw tighten. 'But maybe I wanted to go out with him?'

Deana folded her arms. 'Guy like that? He doesn't even actually like you. He just wants to be the one that gets you. You get me?'

I didn't, and I wasn't sure whether that was funny or really annoying.

'Emma, you're the fittest girl in the school,' Deana said bluntly.

'Shut up!' I gave her a shove.

'You are, though. And that's why all the guys like you, and that's why Lainy can't kick your head in even though she really wants to,' she told me, grinning.

'I thought everyone reckons I'm stuck up,' I said.

'They do,' she said. 'But also fit.'

I'm not a big-head, but I had a feeling she was right. Guys were different with me from how they were with most other girls. They buzzed around me, trying to get my attention. No one had actually asked me out before, though.

That afternoon when I got home, I plonked down on my bed, grabbed the little mirror off my dresser, and had a proper look at myself. My nose was small, which I liked; my eyes were big and a warm brown colour. My lips were red even without lipstick, and my teeth were straight. The best bit of me, I decided then, was my hair. Long and soft with waves, it framed my face really well. I never took hair straighteners to it like everyone else. I'd always loved my curls.

I started to secretly think that maybe looking the way I did was my way to the life I'd always dreamed about.

*

The next day, I ignored Carlos and he ignored me. He was fit, but I wasn't interested. He'd been with quite a few girls from my year, I'd heard. His attention had been nice, and it did make me think about myself a bit differently, but I didn't need that drama.

Speaking of which – in Drama class that afternoon, Elis Turner had been mucking about like usual and got a detention for talking back to the teacher.

'Elis's gonna get expelled if he's not careful,' Deana said as we walked home. She and Elis were friends. They were both sprinters and had a whole 'respect for each other' thing going on because of Athletics club. 'If I spoke to a teacher like that, and they called my mum and dad, I would be so dead, Emma. I swear, like proper in the ground, headstone: "Here lies Deana Khalili. Died of rudeness to the teacher".'

I laughed. 'Shut up. I've met your mum, she's so nice.'

Deana said, 'We're Iraqi though. You just don't mess.'

'But you're not. You live in England now, you're English.'

Deana pulled a face. 'Yeah, but my mum and dad ain't. Their culture says what's right or wrong, that don't bend. In my culture, if you're rude to a teacher, you are dead. And by "culture" I mean my mum and dad. My dad makes me turn the TV off if people start kissing.'

I chuckled again. 'Would they be OK with you having a boyfriend?'

Deana nodded. 'Oh yeah, they'd be fine with that. No problem at all. I can have as many boyfriends as I want – as long as I don't mind being, as I explained earlier, *dead*.'

'But are your mum and dad cool with you being friends with Elis? Do they worry he's your boyfriend?'

'Nah. I can have friends at school or whatever, but I couldn't be caught hanging out with him after school.'

'So they don't know you're friends like that?'

'Exactly.'

'So what about if he calls you or messages?'

'I stored his number in my phone under "Emma".' She grinned. 'They think you call me a lot!'

'That's genius!' I laughed.

Deana was still smiling, but she sighed a bit, too. 'It's survival. When your parents are really strict because they want you to be a good girl, what they are actually doing is teaching you how to lie.'

'You really like him, don't you?' I said. 'To lie to your parents, I mean?'

She shrugged. 'He's all right.'

I raised an eyebrow. 'So why does he get so annoying at school?'

'He can't read,' Deana said casually. 'When he looks at words written on a page, he can't work out what they say.'

'Wow,' I said. 'Like, you mean maybe there's something wrong with him?'

'Rude!'

'No! I mean, maybe he's dyslexic or something, and the teachers don't know.'

Deana shrugged again, and explained that Elis wasn't thick, or dyslexic, or anything else. It was just that getting in trouble was better than people finding out. When she said that, it made sense that he was so loud at school.

There was something about Elis that Deana related to. I could see that. She wore a hijab, and so people assumed she was going to be narrow-minded and ultra-religious, missing what a laugh she was and how she never judged anyone. Elis was a tall Black kid who mucked about in class, and so teachers assumed he was a troublemaker, not a kid who needed help with something he was ashamed of. People looked at Deana and thought 'religious nutjob'. Looked at Elis and thought 'thug'.

But I learned more about him chatting to Deana that day, and I realised something. You can't skim over people like that. If you do, you miss gold.

FIVE

Mum's idea of the Perfect Man had always been someone rich.

'You know, before your dad, there was a fella who wanted to marry me, had his own plumbing business. Minted, he was.'

Mum regularly told me about the Plumber. She ended up going off him because 'he chewed his food so noisily and didn't have much of a neck'. It was her cautionary tale. Dad was good-looking but a nightmare. The neckless Plumber 'would have looked after us properly'.

'Except,' I told her, 'he wouldn't have looked after *us* exactly, would he? You had me with Dad, so I wouldn't exist with the Plumber. You'd have a different kid with no neck.'

'Smart arse,' Mum said, smiling. It was good to have a laugh with her again. We hadn't done enough of that.

I gave her arm a squeeze. 'We don't need some man to come along and sort things out, you know. I'm gonna make my *own* money, like Suze does, and get a flat that *I* pay for.'

'Suze isn't young and gorgeous like you, my darling. You can aim higher – get yourself a man who will treat you like a queen and you won't have to lift a finger.'

'And treat *you* like the Queen Mum, eh? I know what you're up to, Mother.' I waggled my finger at her.

Suze had bought her little house on the other end of our estate off the council the moment she could afford to. That's what I wanted. I could get a good job, I knew I could. I was OK at school, got decent grades if I put the effort in and stayed in the library to use the internet. I might even be able to get some A-levels.

'Suze has done it all without a man, Mum,' I told her. 'It is possible.'

Mum gave me a look. 'Suze is different.'

Suze being trans is something we hardly ever talked about. I could tell Mum wasn't comfortable discussing it.

'I know, but that's not the point,' I said. '*She's* never had a partner with money, has she? She's done it all by herself. She didn't have to have sex with someone to get a house.'

Mum was folding clothes and threw a pair of knickers at my head. 'I don't want to talk about Suze's love life with you, thank you very much.'

I had started to feel like Mum saw my looks as a meal ticket. I'd made the mistake of telling her about Carlos, and although she'd said Deana was right to block it, I got a sense that she was also kind of proud.

'Just don't be flattered by any old Tom, Dick or Harry,' she said. 'Aim higher.'

Mum, without having anything to be snobby about, is actually a gigantic snob. 'Boys round here think mugging and drug dealing are career options,' she loved to say. 'You walk nice and talk nice and you will never want for anything. Men like a bit of class.'

Mum's favourite film was *Gentlemen Prefer Blondes*. We'd watched it together so often, I knew it off by heart. There's a bit where Marilyn Monroe meets her boyfriend's rich dad and he accuses her of being a gold digger, and Marilyn says to him, 'Don't you know that a man being rich is like a girl being pretty? You might not marry a girl just because she's pretty, but, my goodness, doesn't it help?' Mum would rewind that part again and again. She's not subtle, my mum. She got Marilyn Monroe to raise me.

Mum was really into the Kardashians, too. Never missed their show.

'They are so beautiful, so . . . *perfect*,' she would say.

I'd tell her, 'Mum, you know none of it's natural. They've got money; they pay to look like that.'

But that didn't matter to Mum. 'So what? Marilyn wasn't

born blonde. She wasn't born a superstar. She used to be plain old Norma Jean, and look what she made of herself. You won't be plain old Emma Lyons one day. You'll be up there with the best of them.'

Mum had this idea that one day I'd get 'discovered'. Much as I tried not to get too sucked in, she put that idea in my head, too. I took the piss, but I kind of believed her. I believed there would be a time when the right bloke would come along and help me make my dreams come true.

Mum's nightmare was that I'd get pregnant by some loser, though, and that would be that. 'If you get up the duff with some rat-faced boy, then it's game over,' she said to me as she finished folding the clothes. 'Nothing against rats, but I don't want you to end up like me. Stuck with a baby before you've had a chance to live your life.'

I smiled at her. 'Hello? You know I *am* that baby you were stuck with, yeah?'

She tucked the clothes in the drawer and gave me a reassuring squeeze. 'I know, darling, and I don't regret it for a second. But it's been hard. You know that. I don't want you to be shoplifting nappies because you can't afford to buy them. I want you to have everything you want in life. Nice clothes, dinner at fancy places, a man who'll look after you. I want you to have all the things I never had.'

I couldn't argue with that. I didn't want to end up like Mum either.

All mums think their kids deserve better than what they had. My mum and Deana's mum had that much in common. Mum thought I was too good for the boys around the estate – and Deana's mum, it turned out, thought Deana was too good to hang out with the likes of me.

She had been nice enough to me when I went round, the one time I did. But I was never invited again. I didn't do anything wrong when I went there. I didn't pee on the carpet or anything, but Deana was weird when I mentioned going round again and so I left it.

Then Deana told me her parents found out that my mum had been accused of murder.

'No offence,' she said awkwardly, 'but they are really traditional. A whiff of any trouble and they freak out. We can hang out at school, but I can't come to yours and you can't come to mine.'

I was hurt, but I didn't tell Deana that. What could she do? At least I still had her in school.

But even that was about to change.

Me and Deana had got into trouble. Not massively, just got told off for coming back late from games. The games field was a ten-minute walk up the hill from our school, and a few times, we were caught coming back late because we'd stopped off at the sweet shop and Deana spent ages choosing whether to buy a Coke or a Fanta. Seriously, it was the only reason we were ever late, and it wasn't even really my fault.

Deana was weird with me in our detention, but a teacher was there so I couldn't ask why.

'I'm not walking home, my dad's picking me up,' she said when we finished.

'Can I get a lift then?' I asked.

Then Deana just came out with it. 'To be honest, Em, my mum doesn't want me to hang out with you no more. Not even at school. I don't want them to know we were together.'

'What?'

Deana looked embarrassed. This wasn't one of her jokes. I'd never seen her so completely and utterly without a smile or spark. She said it again. 'I can't hang out with you no more. My mum and dad said, and I have to respect them.'

'What are you on about? All because of one detention?'

She shook her head. 'No. They say you're a bad influence. All that stuff with your dad. They told me ages ago I couldn't talk to you, and now they've found out I have been still, and . . .'

I felt like crying, but I held the tears in. I *needed* Deana. I couldn't bear the idea of us not being friends.

'But . . . you can be friends with who you like, right? Like Elis. They can't tell you not to talk to me at *all*,' I said, sounding desperate.

'They can,' Deana whispered. 'They're my mum and dad. I have to respect that. You don't understand, but I have to. You don't get how strict they are. Things have been really bad, and I don't want to lie to them any more or it'll be even worse.'

She was walking away. I was really trying not to cry now but tears came anyway.

'Deana!' I called after her, and she broke into a run, heading to her dad's car. I saw her get in without looking in my direction, and he drove her away.

I stayed there like an idiot for a while. I didn't have a tissue, so I wiped my snot on my sleeve. Half of me expected Deana would get her dad to turn back, lean out of the car window, burst out laughing and say, 'Ha! You fell for it!' She didn't.

I'll see Deana tomorrow, I told myself. Everything would go back to normal.

But the next day, Deana ghosted me. She looked past me when I came near and looked away when I tried to talk to her. I had lunch on my own. She had lunch with some girls from her Maths club. Even Elis was weird with me. He was always more her friend than mine anyway, and now, although he didn't blank me, he didn't really talk to me either. I couldn't believe she was friends with him still, and not me.

The second I got in after school, I cried like a baby. I didn't want to explain what had happened, and what Deana had said. Mum gets enough of people thinking we're scum. But the crying made it pretty obvious something was up.

'She won't talk to me any more, Mum. Not even "hello" in the corridor. I had to have lunch on my own; I haven't got any other friends. She was it!' I properly sobbed like I was five.

Mum sat me down, still wearing her cleaning overalls, and got me some water. She wiped my face with her palm. 'So you did nothing at all; you never said anything to upset her?'

I shook my head cautiously.

Mum cuddled me. I had a feeling she sensed why Deana had changed her mind about us being friends. But she just said, 'You go and wash your face, my darling. I'm going to make us some sandwiches, with crisps, and we're gonna sit and eat our tea in front of the TV tonight, OK?'

I nodded.

'It's Friday night after all,' Mum said in her 'cheer up' voice.

I went to the bathroom, feeling like my mum was the only person I had in the whole world.

*

The next day was Saturday, and as usual we went to the market to get some supplies in – everything there was cheaper than in the supermarket.

We saw Deana's mum by one of the stalls. That's when I realised that Mum wasn't as chilled about the whole thing as she had made out. When I definitely understood that she had an idea what had happened.

Deana wasn't with her mum, thank god, but Mum went up and said, 'Hello, Ashraf, isn't it? I'm Mary, Emma's mum. We've met before, just the once, when I picked Emma up from your house.'

Deana's mum smiled awkwardly, nodded. She had a pretty face, like Deana's, and was clutching the hand of one of Deana's little brothers. She tried to walk off, the stiff smile still on her face. Mum, though, stood in her way.

'May I ask why my daughter isn't good enough to be friends with yours?' she said at normal volume.

Deana's mum looked horrified. I did too, I think. She gripped Deana's little brother's hand tighter, said something quietly to him in Arabic and went to walk away again, this time making it around my mum and hurrying away.

Mum lost it then. 'You know what?' she shouted after her. 'We've been nice to you, we welcomed you here, and you treat my girl like this?'

'Mum!' I tried to move her away. The little kid turned back to us, looking scared. People were staring.

'This is MY country! How dare you judge me?' Mum shouted. 'Why don't you fuck off home?'

I wanted the ground to swallow me up when she said that. Mum wasn't a racist. She really wasn't. Except when she was upset. Then she might have got a bit racist . . .

The whole thing didn't exactly help with our image. Loads of people were about, and word got round. By teatime the story on the estate was that Mum had tried to murder a Muslim woman by a fruit stall.

Deana stayed well and truly away from me after that. She hung out with another Muslim girl called Shadi who no way had the same sense of humour as Deana. There was no chance Deana was having as much fun with her as she did with me.

Now I flitted about between different groups of people at school, never quite fitting in. I didn't get on with anyone like I got on with Deana. 'I'm the only one who likes you,' she had joked once. I think she was right – or at least she was the only one who really got me. But it turned out it was easy for her to turn her back on me. Just like everyone else.

SIX

A few weeks later, Mum opened the package with dog turd in it.

I heard her scream, and I came running out of the kitchen. I'd been slathering butter on to some slices of bread, sprinkling sugar over it to make a sandwich, and usually nothing can put me off my food. Just as I bit into it, the smell hit me. Even something as delicious as a sugar sandwich tastes vile if you've just sniffed two nostrilfuls of dog poo.

'Jesus Christ!' Mum cried, pushing past me, shoving it into a bin bag and taking it straight to the rubbish chute. 'What sickos would do this?'

The smell was still lingering, even after she had thrown it away. The stench of dog shit filled the whole flat.

'Who would have done this?' Mum kept raging, like I would have a clue.

'Someone at your school? Deana! I bet it was Deana or one of her lot.'

'What do you mean, "her lot", Mum? Deana wouldn't do this, neither would her family.' I absolutely knew they wouldn't. 'Anyway, they're Muslim. Dogs are haram. They don't touch dogs, let alone the poo.'

She looked at me like I was speaking Martian, her shoulders sagging in defeat. 'It's never going to end, Emma,' she said. She sank down at our little kitchen table, tears rolling down her cheeks. 'Never.'

*

'It'll be bored little twats on the estate with nothing better to do, babe,' Suze told Mum when she came over, like she always did now on a Friday evening. She was baking cakes in our oven: the only way, she said, to get the shit stink out of our noses.

Suze, it turned out, had been through this herself.

'It makes you paranoid,' she said, 'when you don't know who did it. Makes you suspicious of everyone.'

After that, I stopped saying hello even to the handful of people around town that I usually said hello to. I ran home from the bus stop just to get indoors. How could someone like me get off this estate? There was no way I could learn to live with it. I wanted nothing more than to get away.

I spent hours on my phone, or as long as my credit lasted, looking at posts of girls with expensive clothes and perfect boobs, flat bellies and sculpted faces, girls with hundreds of thousands of followers. They all looked the same, all doing the same poses.

I didn't have a bikini to pose in, so I stood in my underwear in front of the full-length mirror on the inside of my wardrobe, sucked my belly in and pushed my boobs out. I smiled, which is something those girls didn't do. I shook out my hair so it flowed around my face. I looked good. Then I leaned back too far, trying to see all of myself in the mirror. One stumble, and I fell and whacked my head on the door handle behind me.

'You all right, Emma?' Mum shouted from the front room.

'Yeah!' I shouted back quickly, before she could come in.

Beauty was a talent. Wasn't that what Mum always told me? 'It's not all about how pretty you are, or how perfect your body is. It's how you present yourself.' Could I stand out online? Could that be my way of getting some money? Getting out of here?

Mum definitely wanted to leave now. But she was still trying to think of any other option than Nan's.

'We could ask the council to transfer us?' she considered out loud. 'But god knows how long that would take or where they would put us. They could put us anywhere in the country!'

I didn't know any other part of the country. Anywhere had to be better than here, though.

Sheila upstairs was upset we were thinking about leaving. 'Don't let them drive you away, loves. This is your home.'

'But what kind of a home is it if we don't feel safe?' Mum replied in despair.

'It's all right for Sheila,' Mum said to me when we came downstairs. 'She's an old lady. She has no kids; she's had her life; she hasn't got to build a future for anyone, has she?'

'She's not that old,' I said. Mum was being a bit harsh on Sheila. I could see that she and Martin didn't want us to leave, and it was nice to be wanted by *someone*. But Mum was so wrapped up in what was going on, she didn't see that Sheila needed us to look after. She and Martin didn't have much else.

'We can't stay, though, Emma, can we?' Mum said. 'This place, this place – it drags you down. It's like quicksand. We've got to go before we disappear. Before it swallows us.'

*

At school there was a note in my locker from Deana. It just said, *I heard about the dog shit. I'm sorry.* A big whoosh of happiness went through me when I saw it. Was this her saying she wanted us to be friends again?

I went to find her after my class but she didn't want to talk to me. 'Look, I just heard what happened,' she said, 'and I felt sorry for you, OK? Nothing's changed. You gotta leave me alone.'

I walked away, feeling so stupid. Later, I ripped up her dumb note.

*

For my sixteenth birthday, Mum gave me clothes, really nice clothes: a pair of dark denim jeans, two cute T-shirts and a black furry hoodie. Not cheap from the market; from a proper shop.

'You got to make the effort to attract a different sort of bloke, Emma,' she said. 'Clothes say a lot about a person. Mine say I've got to lose half a stone,' she added with a chuckle.

It turned out that one woman she cleaned for had two girls a bit older than me. When she saw a pile of clothes the woman had set aside for the charity shop, stuff her daughters had grown out of, Mum begged it off her. After that, I got all of the sisters' old clothes.

'Just don't tell anyone where I get them,' Mum said.

She didn't want people to think she was dressing me in second-hand clothes. She was funny about stuff like that. I wasn't sure how to feel about it myself, but the clothes were really nice, and they fitted me well. So I wore clothes that 'Isadora and Allegra' had grown out of. Really good stuff, like from Next and Zara. They looked like they'd never been worn, to be fair.

The woman, a doctor, even gave Mum a few bits and pieces of her old designer stuff. Mum was the only woman on the estate with a Mulberry handbag. It was old, but still. She made sure everyone knew she had it, even though she had to point the logo out to Sheila and Suze, or to the one or two strangers in a shop who might compliment it. Then she'd have to explain what it was and how much it cost new.

'For god's sake,' Suze said, laughing. 'Why do you even bother carrying that huge thing around? Just show people a screenshot with the price on it.'

'You got to look the part, then you'll BE the part,' Mum said.

'Honestly, Emma,' Suze said to me, rolling her eyes. 'One tatty old Mulberry bag and your mum thinks she's Kim Kardashian.'

But I understood now. The dream Mum had of having something more, a better life.

*

Nan was still FaceTiming us, but Mum's phone was getting old and in need of an update, so it kept cutting out. I wished we had broadband.

Nan couldn't understand why were were still on the estate. 'Just move in with me, Mary. It's not ideal, but we'd make room.'

'Why *can't* we live with Nan?' I asked my mum after Nan had rung off. It was a conversation we'd been having for years, and I still didn't have the answer I wanted.

Mum sniffed. 'She's only asking because she feels she has to, and I am not a charity case. We'll work something out.'

Mum's plan was to find a man to take care of us.

I knew she was hatching her plan when she asked me to help do her make-up and choose an outfit for the club – which was actually just a bar in the community hall they had every Saturday with cheap drinks. Suze helped out behind the bar sometimes. Then off she and Suze went.

Mum looked good, and I knew she wasn't going just to keep Suze company.

Mum was always worrying about money. We never had enough for the heating. Going to bed wearing our coats was normal. It was obvious that she was trying to find a bloke to take the pressure off. I don't think she cared about being in love. She just wanted a man with money.

Going to the club became a regular thing. I didn't like being in the flat on my own, but I never said. I liked hearing the gossip when she got back.

Soon she met some bloke Terry at the club, an older guy. He drove a lorry, and he didn't live on the estate.

'Look!' she said, all excited when she got back from an evening out with him. She excitedly held a little polystyrene box up in the air. It held two slices of fancy pizza she'd saved for me from their meal.

'He took me to a lovely place,' she said, sitting beside me on the sofa. 'Really thin pizzas. I wish I could have saved you

60

some pudding but it was sticky toffee and we just shared one between us.' Her eyes were glowing like sharing a pudding was the best thing anyone had ever done with her.

'Watch out, Mum! Next he'll be asking to hold your hand,' I said through a mouthful of pizza. I was really hungry. I'd only had cereal for dinner, since there was nothing much to eat in the house.

Mum smiled coyly. 'I wanted to ask you about that. How would you feel if he stayed over here one night?'

The vision of Mum having sex wasn't one I wanted to encourage. Plus, there was something about my mum feeling she had to support us by finding a man that felt weird, uncomfortable. Like she shouldn't have to do all of that. Like I should be pulling my weight, finding some way to help put food in the fridge. I shrugged.

'Fine. I don't care,' I told her, but it sort of felt like a lie. I polished off the pizza quickly. 'Is he your boyfriend now?'

'Not exactly,' she said. 'It's complicated, darling. I don't really want anyone to know.'

A couple of days later, I saw a message from Suze on Mum's phone screen, asking about Mum's 'sugar daddy' with a laughing emoji. I only kind of knew what it meant.

Turns out it didn't really matter. Mum's secret didn't last long.

'You slag! Keep your mucky, murdering hands to yourself!'

The shout felt like a shove at our backs. We were coming back from the shops. I didn't turn around; neither did Mum.

The way things had been for us, I think she would have been *more* surprised if someone had shouted 'Good morning!' at her.

'Who is it?' I asked Mum under my breath as she marched forward fast, and I quickened my pace to follow.

'Terry's wife.'

I reared back. 'Jesus, Mum! What have you been up to?'

Terry's wife wasn't on her own. Other women were with her. They all shouted horrible names at Mum.

'Just hold your head up high and walk on, Emma,' Mum told me. Like she always did.

I don't think she saw Terry again after that. She didn't mention him anyway, and I didn't ask. Even more people hated us now. She stopped going to the club.

People knowing your business is hard. 'Hey! Emma!' boys would shout at me. 'Are you a slag like your mum?' And I would just keep walking, feeling their eyes on me, terrified they would follow me.

I had to do something. I was sixteen now; I could do something to help. If Mum wasn't going to move us to Nan's, then I'd have to work out a way to get money so we could go somewhere else. It was like I used to say to Deana – I could get a job. I don't know why I hadn't thought about it before. There were Saturday roles going at the supermarket, and some girls I knew swept hair at the hairdressers. I applied for a few jobs, but the people who already knew us wouldn't give me the time of day.

'It's already been filled,' the manager at Hair There and Everywhere said, not looking me in the eye.

'The sign says you need someone.'

She looked at me and said, 'There isn't a job for *you* here.' Then she pretended to be busy at the computer.

The hairdressers and a couple of the customers were glancing over at me. I'd spent two hours doing my hair, getting it perfect before I went in. This wasn't fair. Resisting the urge to swear at her, I swished my hair over my shoulder and left.

The supervisor at the supermarket barely even interviewed me. He was about fifty, quite small and skinny, with receding hair and a long ponytail tied low and lying limply between his shoulder blades. He took me into a tiny office at the back, but we didn't stop there. He led me through some more doors and into what looked like a storeroom.

'You have any experience?' he asked me when I sat down. He was staring at my boobs. 'In a supermarket, I mean,' he added, smiling really creepily.

I told him I didn't, but he said I could start straight away. 'I'll have to train you myself today, OK?'

'OK,' I said cautiously. I wanted to start earning some money, so I stayed, in spite of the weird vibe he was giving off.

During the 'training', he kept putting his hands on my waist. 'Try and reach up, that's it. You need to put all the ketchup on that top shelf.'

He was grossing me out. When he left me alone for a bit, I said to the other woman working in my aisle, 'He's a bit of a letch, isn't he?'

She was older than me and didn't really react, like she was wondering why I was even talking to her. I had to tell myself to focus on the money I'd make.

After he came back from lunch, the supervisor gave me a crate of sweetcorn tins to stack. As he started to walk off, I felt his hand on my bum, just slightly, just faintly brushing it. I didn't imagine it.

'Oi!' I shouted.

He just kept walking. He didn't even turn around. A few people looked up, hearing me shout. My face was burning. Sod the pay, I just wanted to get out.

I grabbed my coat and left.

I didn't have many more job options. I could have asked in other shops, but after what had happened at the hairdressers, I didn't feel confident. *There must be another way*, I thought. Mum worked so hard, but I needed to earn too. Problem was – how?

I couldn't stand another day of school. I was so lonely, and all the teachers could talk about was how important this year was – Year Eleven, our GCSEs. Every day there was a fight – not just the boys, but the girls too. I felt vulnerable, on my own. Me and Deanna had been a gang, but these days I had no one. The boys still made comments when I walked past, staring at me, trying to brush up against me. Plus when the teachers asked me a question, I usually knew the answer. Fatal. 'Swot!' I'd hear in a whisper. It was difficult to blend into the background. More and more, all I wanted to do was disappear.

Every time I walked through the estate, my insides froze until I was in our flat. The words 'Nice tits!' followed me everywhere, no matter what I wore. Even if they didn't say anything, men and boys stared, and every part of me tensed up as I went past. Anxiety sat in my stomach every day after school till I got in. Back in the flat, with Mum, and Sheila and Mike upstairs, I could start breathing again.

Who wanted to live like this? How were we going to get out of this mess?

SEVEN

Then there was that afternoon in October.

It was already dark as I came home from school. My breath clouded in the air – it was freezing, and everyone was indoors, except for three boys hanging around in the stairwell near my flat. I didn't know them, but I could tell they knew exactly who I was. Like they had come to find me, specifically. They looked about the same age as me, maybe seventeen – but I knew that boys that age can be as strong as men. And *they* knew I had no dad around to run out and hammer them. Whatever Dad had been like at home, he'd never have let anyone else touch us. That had been for him alone.

When they saw me, I heard one of them say, 'Here she comes.'

My blood froze. Instinct told me this would be bad. Very bad.

They stank of booze, one still holding a bottle. Quickly they surrounded me in the stairwell, blocking my path.

'Oi oi, girl! You going to go up without saying hello?' one of them said.

I shook my head.

'C'mon babe, all I want is a hello. You can do that, can't you? It's basic manners,' he said, smirking.

The other two laughed. Two were behind me and one in front, trapping me.

'You shy? Tell you what, if you can't say hello then you can just give us a kiss, Emma. Just one little kiss . . .' – the one in front smirked at his friends – '. . . *each*, and then you can go.'

They knew my name. And where I lived. I was in trouble.

Before I understood what was happening, the two behind me grabbed my shoulders, restraining me. I screamed, suddenly finding my voice. There was a hand on my boob, a hand between my legs . . . hands, everywhere. All over me. Hot, sour breath in my face as I squirmed while one of them tried to kiss me.

I shouted, 'GET OFF!' and 'HELP!' over and over again, my voice echoing up the stairwell, like my dad's voice used to when he'd storm off, calling me and Mum names. I screamed as loud as I could, until one of the boys slapped me, slamming me against the wall. Another one hissed in my ear, telling me to shut up. I felt his saliva fleck against the side of my face, and tears blurred my vision.

But I did shut up. I just cried silently, still wriggling and kicking out. There were hands gripping my wrists, one on my leg, trying to keep me still. Then another hand was trying to tug my jeans down. I twisted and turned as much as I could, whimpering, my voice somehow forced into silence, but it was three against one. I couldn't fight them off. Panic broke me out in a cold sweat, despite the frosty air.

Suddenly, I heard footsteps clattering down the stairs – my mum's slippers slapping against the concrete. She came bombing down the stairwell, throwing herself at the blokes like a mad thing, screaming and hitting out at them. With a wave of relief I felt them release their grip and watched them run off like startled cats.

Then I was on the floor, crumpled into a heap. The minute I felt Mum's arms around me, my body started shaking uncontrollably with the cold and the shock. I heard myself crying just out of relief that she was there. Mum got me to my feet and took me upstairs.

'I knew something was up before I even heard you scream.' Mum was holding me on the sofa now, stroking my hair. 'I felt it. This dread.'

'What if they come back, Mum?' I asked, hiccupping with sobs. I clutched the sugary cup of tea she'd made me. 'They know where I live.'

'They won't. And even if they do, we won't be here.'

I looked up, sniffing hard. Her eyes were cold and hard and flat as stones.

'Now stop crying and get your things,' she added.

Before I could respond, she got up, went into her room and grabbed the big case out from under her bed, storming back to the living room and holding it up.

'I've had it, Emma, I've had it,' she kept hissing over and over again, grabbing things off the laundry dryer by the window and throwing them into the suitcase, returning to her room, grabbing another armful of stuff. 'We're done here.'

It felt like an electric charge had suddenly gone through me. I pulled things of mine out of the case that Mum had just shoved in there, replacing them with things I actually wanted. Bob the Penguin, a cuddly toy from when I was little. My favourite jumper and a little framed photo of me and Mum when I was a tiny baby. The clothes she'd given me for my birthday . . .

We packed frantically in a short time.

'You're not going to tell the police about what happened to me, are you?' I said as Mum did up her rucksack. 'I don't want to talk to the police again.'

'No, I'm bloody well not. The last thing we need, Emma, is more police round here. We'll just get out of here. We'll go to your nan's. It'll be safe there.'

We didn't even say goodbye to Sheila or Martin or Suze. No time. Didn't even cross our minds. We just heaved our bags to the lift, then carried them to the bus stop. My heart beat like mad while we waited. I was still terrified those boys would show up again. Would they do it to another girl? I didn't want to think about that.

We had a bag of clothes each. That was it. Mum had filled the case with pictures and other bits she didn't want to leave, plus her rucksack. I had my big rucksack, but that was basically it. A few bags to show for our whole lives. Mum left the framed pictures of Dad still hanging back there on the hall wall.

I didn't care because we were off to Nan's estate on the other side of London and that was all that mattered. I didn't care if we never came back. I was getting away from my school, away from my estate, away from my long-lost Deana.

Away from all the memories of my dad.

EIGHT

Three buses to Nan's. We were sweating, even though it was cold out, from heaving our bags, both our hearts pounding like we were still running. We sat on the bottom deck, people getting all tut-tut with us because our bags took up all the space in the luggage area.

At last, we were going to be free. Away from Elmsworth, Mum and I would be normal. When we got to Nan's area, nobody would know us except for Nan and Auntie Jean and our cousins. And, I supposed, anyone who put *man pushed off 12th floor by wife* into a search engine. But I didn't want to think about that. Not when we'd finally escaped.

Nan's place was a maisonette. It had stairs inside, so as far as I was concerned it was a house. When I was a kid I had dreamed of living somewhere with stairs, and now here I was. It had three bedrooms and a tiny room Nan called 'the west wing', which was too small for a bed, so Nan kept her iron and ironing board there. She took in people's ironing and earned a bit of cash in hand like that. Nan had her own room, my cousins shared, and Auntie Jean had the third.

The minute we rang the bell, Nan had the door open, hands on her hips as she looked at us for a moment with a smile before welcoming us in. Mum had rung her from the bus. We were to sleep in the living room, Mum on the sofa and I on a fold-up mattress thing on the floor. I didn't care. I was just relieved we were there.

Auntie Jean came down the stairs and gave me a big hug. 'My god, is this Emma? You're all grown up! Look at you!' she squealed. 'You're a woman!'

You wouldn't know Auntie Jean and Mum were sisters. Not just in their looks, but their personalities. Jean was all peroxide blonde hair and 'OMG!', with bright-blue, eighties eyeliner. She was thinner than Mum, really thin, and she smoked all the time. She was always either putting one out or lighting one up. She was hyper.

'Jade! Becca!' she shouted out of the open door towards the rest of the flat, cigarette in hand, dancing from one foot to the other.

Nan looked at me and said, 'She's got fireworks up her bum, that one.'

Mum snorted.

Jean shouted again for her daughters. 'Come and see your cousin Emma! They've come to stay!' she yelled, then barely lowered her voice as she turned to me, exhaling a plume of smoke. 'So how are you, my darling? God, I look a mess. Do I look a mess? I've not had me roots done. If I'd known I'd be seeing you I would've made an effort, you know. You get here all right on the bus with all your stuff? Where are those girls? *Jade! Becca!*'

Auntie Jean was the sort of person who asked questions and never waited for your answer. Jade and Becca eventually came in. We sat awkwardly in the front room with Mum's and my bags taking up most of the floor space. They were in their twenties, and both had blonde hair that they'd dyed lavender. They were very quiet. I couldn't work out if they were just like that, or if it was because they didn't want us there, or because Auntie Jean literally didn't let anyone else get a word in ever.

'Why don't you show your cousin Emma your room?' Auntie Jean said.

'Because we're not five?' Jade snapped.

Nan chuckled sarcastically. 'Don't worry, Emma. I never get much out of them two either.'

Nan wasn't the knitting and baking type of grandmother. She was the smoking, drinking and swearing sort. My grandad, by all accounts, had been the same. He'd died a long time ago in a car crash, driving himself home from the pub after a heavy session, leaving Nan to raise Auntie Jean and my mum on her own.

'Two kids on my own, no man, no money.' She was telling the story again. 'And here you all are, back under my wing, eh?'

'We know you sorted us all out, Nan. You tell us that ten times a day,' Becca finally said.

Nan ignored her. 'I never had a nan to take me in. You should be grateful!'

That first night, Nan was making us all spaghetti when Mum told her about the lads in the stairwell. She'd only told her on the phone that we needed to get away, but not why. I felt a flush of heat spread across my face as Mum told the story. Especially when Nan looked me up and down and said, 'Put less on show, love. Men can't help themselves around a bit of flesh.'

'Oh my god, Nan!' I spluttered. 'That's got nothing to do with it!'

Nan looked unconvinced. 'You can't dangle a lamb chop in front of a lion and expect it not to bite.'

I blinked away angry tears. Was she saying this was my fault? I opened my mouth again, but Mum gave me a look that said not to push it – not when we needed somewhere to stay right now. But I was fuming.

'I was dressed normally when those boys did what they did, Nan,' I said, looking down at the kitchen table, my jaw clenched.

Auntie Jean must've seen the tears jump up in my eyes. 'Oh, Emma,' she said. 'Your nan's not exactly up to speed with the whole *Me Too* thing.'

'Oi!' Nan said. 'I'm not a bleeding idiot.' She turned to me, her eyes softening. 'I'm just saying count your blessings and enjoy how gorgeous you are. One day you'll be an old bag like me and no man will look at you.'

'It wasn't just wolf-whistling, you know,' Mum said quietly, finally deciding to stick up for me, sort of.

Nan sighed. 'All right, all right. Men are beasts, is what I'm saying. It's better not to encourage them.'

I couldn't handle this. I headed out of the kitchen and down the short corridor to the front door, letting myself out of the flat. A few steps away, there was a patch of a greenery with a bench. I sat on it, tears running down my face. I wasn't upset – I was angry. And cold. I should have grabbed my jacket.

I texted Deana because there wasn't really anyone else I could reach out to. I knew she wouldn't reply – she never replied – but I wrote anyway.

If you get this Deana, call me. Please? I haven't got another best mate. Please Deana.

Nothing. I was away from the estate, which was definitely a good thing, but I was worried I'd be all alone here.

*

'New school soon, Emma. You need a new identity, and a back story,' Nan said a few days later. Nan watched a lot of crime shows on TV, so I think she had a notion that we were going into Witness Protection or something.

Everyone was crammed around the small kitchen table. Dinner was takeaway pizza courtesy of Mum, who now had not one, not two, but three cleaning jobs. She didn't hang about – she'd gone out and got more work straight away.

'Just don't tell anyone your dad's dead, or how he got that way,' Auntie Jean said to me.

'She can't pretend he's not dead,' Mum said, her eyes flashing at her sister. 'That's too big a lie. It's got to be subtle.'

I arched an eyebrow. 'Like what?'

'Tell them he went away to live on a farm,' said Jean, her thin red gash of a mouth smiling.

She and Nan laughed their heads off. Jade rolled her eyes. Becca looked confused.

'That's what you say when a dog dies and you don't want to upset the kids, you idiot,' Jade told Becca helpfully.

Becca looked even more confused. 'You said Flash went to live on a farm.'

'Flash weren't a dog. Flash was a tortoise,' Nan offered.

'So? He still went to a farm so he'd have more space.' Becca looked upset now. 'You said.'

'Sorry to break it to you, my darling,' Jean said. 'But that tortoise never woke up from hibernation. You were only small. I didn't want to upset you.'

Becca pushed her plate away. 'That's put me right off my food.'

Jade laughed. 'Why? It's not tortoise you're eating, it's pizza.'

Then Becca and Jade's 'Shut up!' and 'No, you shut up!' battle started.

'Both of you shut up!' Nan shouted at them. 'This ain't about tortoises or pizza. This is Emma's life. It's important we handle it right.'

Everyone was quiet.

'Heart attack?' said Jean suddenly.

'Not bad,' said Nan.

'Wouldn't a car crash be better?' Jade chimed in. She lit up a cigarette and leaned back in her chair, not touching her dinner.

'Are you gonna have that slice?' Becca asked. Apparently her appetite had suddenly come back.

'Car crash is too dramatic,' Nan said, sliding the pizza off Jade's plate and on to Becca's. 'Heart attack is better. Quick. No questions.'

So it was decided that my dad had died of a heart attack, and not of smashing down on the pavement from our twelfth-floor balcony. I looked at Mum. She was concentrating very hard on a crust she was cutting up, using a knife and fork.

'This is all very morbid. Poor Emma. This is no fun for you, is it love?' said Jean.

'Queen of the understatements, isn't she, your Auntie Jean,' Nan said, poking my shoulder.

Mum rolled her eyes at Jean, then looked at me. 'You're OK, aren't you love? Your nan's right. We can't let people know our business.'

'I'm fine, Mum.'

That word, 'fine', fixes everything. Your head could be hanging off and all you'd need to say would be 'I'm fine!' and everyone would leave you alone.

It was Nan's idea that we change our surname, too. 'You don't want anyone looking you up easily. Change your name and throw them off the scent.'

She was really getting into this. Mum and I loved the soundtrack to *Hamilton,* so it was decided that I was Emma Hamilton now.

Auntie Jean bleached Mum's hair so it was harder to recognise her from all the pictures they'd had of her in the papers. It suited her.

New school, new area, new hair. New start.

It was just as well, because I was going to be the new girl mid-term. Lucky me. Not exactly the easiest way to blend in. The school was called Lammas Upper. It was smarter than my old school. The bricks that made up the huge main building looked new and bright, burnt red.

Being new in school is a tightrope walk. One wrong move and that's it, you're done. It's hell.

I had Becca's old uniform on. I wanted to look the part, but not a try-hard. I wore a tiny bit of make-up, just to cover a few spots and even out my skin. A smear of lip balm, touch of mascara and that was it. I tied my hair back and pulled a few curls around over my face – my 'deliberately messy' look.

On that first day, a girl called Maisie had to show me to each of my classes, then meet me afterwards to take me to my next one. 'It means missing a few minutes of my own classes to make sure you know where you are.' She said it like missing a bit of class was a *bad* thing. I was quickly realising this place was nothing like my old school.

She took me to my form room, where I discovered a girl called Ellie who hated me on sight. Literally, the minute I walked in.

I wore the same white shirt as everyone else, only I hadn't done up the buttons right at the top because I've got boobs and it's uncomfortable, pulling the material too tight.

Ellie clocked me straight away and muttered, 'Slag.' Loud enough for me to hear.

I realised I had a choice. I could be the old Emma Lyons, who'd have hunched her shoulders and scurried away, not wanting any trouble – or the new Emma Hamilton, who held her head up high and stared back. So that's what I did. The trick was not to show fear. No one could actually hear your heart pumping when you were rattled. You thought they could, but they couldn't.

'What you looking at?' Ellie snarled.

After a beat, I calmly looked away.

'Oi! I'm talking to you.' Ellie was in my face now. A few kids looked over to see what was going on. Ellie was putting on a show for them.

I could give a show of my own. I didn't flinch. 'Calm down, princess,' I said.

Calling someone 'princess' when they are angry is a brilliant way to make an enemy for life.

'Good morning class!'

Our teacher, Miss Macey, bustled along at that moment, thank god. Ellie took a step back. I liked Miss Macey straight away. She had long curly red hair that sprang out all over the place, and a big wide smile that never seemed to leave her face. 'Ah, hello! You must be Emma.'

The rest of the morning was a blur of following Maisie, not knowing where I was meant to be while everyone else charged from class to class, knowing the place like the back of their hand. Boys glanced at me, and the bolder, cheekier ones talked to me. Just 'Hello' and 'Are you new?' while their friends watched, ready to laugh and take the piss. I let the good-looking ones chat to me a bit, smiling politely to everybody else.

At lunchtime, Maisie took me to the hall and pointed. 'You're free dinners, right? That's your queue there.'

Maisie was not 'free dinners'. She went to the queue of kids who had money to pay for their lunch. The shiny-haired queue. Maisie flicked her own silky-straight hair a lot, especially around boys.

When we'd got our food, Maisie met me and said, 'Have you made friends to sit with? Mine are over there.'

It wasn't an invitation. She strode over to a table of shiny, flicky-haired girls. For a split second, I could feel tears prickling my eyelids. I quickly blinked them away and forced myself to soften my face.

Everyone in the hall suddenly turned towards the noise of a scuffle at the other side of the hall. Two teachers got up and sorted it all out in a few seconds – it was amazing how quick. The boys were led out without putting up a fight, and the rest of the kids sat back down after a few half-hearted whoops of 'Fight! Fight!'.

The weight on me lifted a little. These kids thought they were tough – they talked loud, they glared hard, they got into these little fights – but they were *nothing* compared to the kids from my old estate. Maybe this would be easier than I thought.

Maisie reappeared with a few of her friends, who all looked me up and down.

'Oh my god! I didn't realise you were on your own!' Maisie said, even though she'd seen me standing there like Johnny No Mates. 'Come out into the yard with us?'

She'd left me by myself, on my first day. You couldn't give people like that a second chance. If you didn't do what they wanted, they'd ditch you again. I wasn't going to be a puppy following Maisie around.

I looked her in the eye. 'Nah. I'm all right.'

'Suit yourself,' she said, flaring her nostrils, and she and her mates all went off in a swish of perfectly ironed hair.

The tables in the canteen were in five long rows. I went over to an empty seat and clattered my tray on to the table with a sigh. Across from me were two girls who I recognised from my form, quietly chatting side by side, eating their packed lunches.

One of them leaned across to me. 'Hey!' she said. 'That lot are fakes.'

Her friend, a pretty red-headed girl with glasses, nodded. 'Total fakes,' she agreed, and mimicked Maisie in a perfect, exaggerated high-pitched voice: 'Oh my goodness! I didn't realise you were on your OWN!'

The first girl, who had brown eyes, amazingly shaped eyebrows and wore a hijab, cracked up. 'I mean, it's your first day, surely you know EVERYBODY here already? I thought it was FINE to dump you by yourself and ignore you while I sat over there with the VIPs.'

I laughed, and she smiled at me. 'I'm Soreya,' she said. 'And this is Matilda. After you've eaten, come to the yard with *us*, if you like.'

And I did.

'So where do you live?'

'Have you got any brothers or sisters?'

'How come you moved?'

Questions came thick and fast from Soreya and Matilda as we headed out into the fresh air of the courtyard. I was careful not to give too much away, but I also didn't want to sound too much like I was hiding anything.

Soreya was Muslim, like Deana, but she was from Somalia. She was tall and her skin was perfect. Not a single spot or mark. Matilda's red hair was tied back into a bunch and she had masses of freckles flicked on her pale face. We bantered and laughed, mostly at Matilda's jokes. These two were all right.

'So what was your old school like?' Matilda asked.

I shrugged. 'Like this one, I suppose. Maybe a bit more rough?'

'Schools are all basically the same, I reckon,' Soreya said. 'Can't wait to get out of here!'

Soreya and Matilda were both in my Biology class after lunch, so we walked to the block together.

'Open your legs! Fertilise your eggs!' some boy hooted as I walked into the class. He was a tall, chubby boy with red cheeks and freckles. I couldn't let this sort of picking and teasing start again. This was my test. I needed to handle it right.

I looked at him, my heart thumping, but made my voice stay calm. 'I don't talk to little virgins.'

He turned purple. Actually *purple*! His friends were howling like monkeys. I walked over to a free desk and sat down, knowing I'd played it just right.

'Respect!' said Soreya as she and Matilda sat down at the table next to me.

This just might work out, I thought. Things were going to be different at this school.

*

Suze was at Nan's when I got back, and I was so relieved to see her.

'Suze!' I shouted, running up to her and giving her a hug.

She'd dyed her hair a bright, vivid postbox red. 'Your mum said it was your first day, so I had to come and say hello. How did it go?'

I pulled a face, but then let it relax. 'It's school. Not too bad though. Oi, I like your hair, suits you.'

Suze caught us up on her news. Her gran, who she didn't really know and who lived in France, had died and left her a bit of money, and she was thinking of leaving social work and starting a business.

'Jesus, how much did she leave you?' I asked.

'Enough to rent the lease of a coffee shop.'

'Blimey,' Nan said, making everyone a cup of tea. 'When I cark it, most you'll get, Emma, will be whatever's left in the freezer.'

'Where's it gonna be, this coffee shop?' Mum asked.

'Dunno,' Suze said. 'I haven't looked yet. But round our way's gonna start changing soon. Young professionals can't afford Hackney. They're moving further east. Elmsworth is gonna be full of hipsters, trust me. They'll want a vegan café.'

'Not sure Elmsworth is ready for a *vegan* café, Suze,' Mum said, chuckling.

'Not yet, no. Right now most people there think vegan is when you don't eat the egg in your scotch egg,' agreed Suze. 'But I promise you, it's going to change. Just the other day I heard someone in the corner shop ask if they sold essential oils.'

'You never!' Mum said dramatically.

When the joking around stopped and we all had a cup of tea sat in front of us, Suze said, 'Everyone is talking about where you've gone, you know. They wondered if you'd been arrested again.'

Mum smiled triumphantly. 'Disappointed to hear the truth, were they?'

'Believe it or not, some people were concerned,' Suze said.

'Nice to know they care,' Mum said sarcastically.

'Well, I care,' Suze said. 'So do Mike and Sheila. Sheila was dead upset you disappeared without saying anything.'

'We couldn't, Suze,' I chimed in, remembering the panic we'd been in. 'We've been in touch since, haven't we, Mum?'

'I know, I know,' Suze soothed. 'They get it. I'm just being selfish because I miss you both.' She gave my hand a squeeze. 'You two were my only friends on that estate. The only people I could stand, apart from Sheila and Mike. You should come back and visit. When you're ready.'

Mum scoffed quietly, then said exactly what I was thinking. 'No way in hell would I set foot back on that estate.'

Suze had brought a tin of cakes that Sheila had made for us. As I ate them, I closed my eyes. I was back on the stairs up to her flat – her warm, cosy flat that always smelled of baking, where everything was calm. Just for a moment I felt that peace. But then I remembered those boys on the stairwell, their hands everywhere . . .

My eyes flew open. I saw us all crammed into the living room, our stuff scattered round us, Auntie Jean coming in to have a go at Mum about something.

No peace here, and certainly no baking, but at least it wasn't Elmsworth.

NINE

On the second day of school, I was still wondering where I was and where I was supposed to be. But I already knew whose voice it was when I heard someone behind me in the form room.

'Here she is; she's got her boobs out for the lads.'

This time I was more prepared for Ellie. 'You jealous, pancakes?' I retorted – and she flew at me. Like proper went for my hair, grabbed it and tried to pull me down. She was small, but strong.

She was in trouble. They didn't stand for that kind of thing at this school, that much I knew.

'Personal remarks about one another's bodies and fighting are not tolerated at Lammas, Ellie!' Miss Macey said when we were hauled into the head teacher's office.

'But she said—' Ellie tried to interject, but Miss Sharma, the head teacher, cut her off, ignoring her protests.

'Our school policy is sharing and reconciling,' she scolded.

So that lunchtime, we had to sit in an empty classroom with Miss Macey eating her sandwiches. I had to tell Ellie how her comments made me feel, and Ellie had to pretend she was sorry.

'I can't change my boobs. I'm proud of them,' I told her. Not words I ever expected to say at school in front of a teacher.

Miss Macey nodded approvingly, dabbing her mouth with a napkin. 'Can you understand, Ellie, what Emma is saying?'

Ellie rolled her eyes. 'Yes, miss. It was just a joke.'

'Did you find it funny, Emma?' Miss Macey asked really calmly, like she was asking, 'Do you like apples, Emma?'

I was used to so much worse than Ellie, but she didn't know that. She didn't know that I wasn't an easy target. She wouldn't have lasted five minutes at Elmsworth. Even though I'd escaped, I was from there, and it had taught me to stand my ground and not be afraid of people like Ellie. And I knew how to play the game with grown-ups.

'I didn't find it funny, miss,' I said, making sure my voice sounded really wounded. 'I found it rude and hurtful.'

Miss Macey smiled reassuringly and reached out to squeeze my hand. As she let go to put the lid on her sandwich box, I gave Ellie a little smirk, because I knew it would make her angry. Her cheeks reddened.

'Great start, very honest,' said Miss Macey. 'Ellie, I'd like you to really *hear* Emma. How else did Ellie's words make you feel?'

I pretended to think for a moment, then said, 'Well . . . I find it pervy, the way she stares at my boobs and comments on them. It makes me feel very uncomfortable, miss.'

'She's so full of shit, miss. How can you believe this crap?' Ellie grabbed her bag off the floor and stormed out of the room.

'Oh dear,' Miss Macey said, watching Ellie leave. 'We'll have to get her mother in. I'm afraid Ellie finds all this very challenging.' She looked at me, blinking gently. 'We act up and get defensive when we feel challenged.'

I tried not to laugh. 'She's going to hate me even more now I've got her in trouble,' I said.

'I don't think she hates you; I think she feels envious of you.' Miss Macey nodded wisely. 'Now off you go, too.'

There was quite a bit of lunchtime left, what with Ellie flouncing off.

'Oi! New girl!' Matilda called out, and beckoned me across the yard to join her and Soreya. 'Heard you got in a fight. On your second day!'

She whooped and high-fived Soreya. She was joking, I knew. Neither was the type to get into fights.

I smiled and said, 'I didn't get into a fight! Ellie attacked me and I stood up for myself. Big difference.'

Soreya was quieter than Matilda, very chilled, very relaxed. 'Ellie's got issues,' she said. 'She's always starting something. Remember when she tried it with me? But I got five brothers. She didn't try that shit again!' She hooted.

'I told Miss Macey she made comments about my boobs like some pervy old bloke, and Ellie went mad and stormed out.'

'Ah, she's jealous of you,' Soreya said. 'She's a jealous person.'

Matilda held out her bag of crisps for me to take some. I hadn't gone in for lunch in the canteen. I didn't want to run the risk of bumping into Ellie after her hissy fit.

'Why would she be jealous of me?' I asked, genuinely baffled.

Matilda cackled. 'Woooo! Look at you fishing! Like you don't know you look like a model.'

'Shut up.'

'Truth. Me and Soreya were saying earlier, weren't we?' She looked at her friend, who nodded. 'You're so pretty, you could be a model.'

'Not catwalk, you're too short for that,' Soreya said with a smile. 'But yeah, you're easily pretty enough. Are you on Insta? You should get followers, then you'll get loads of free stuff.'

'Then give it all to me,' Matilda added. 'What kind of a new friend are you? Get your boobs out on Insta and get me free stuff!'

The three of us became a little group of our own that didn't really fit anywhere else. It began to feel like this school just might be all right.

There were loads of groups of girls. The Sporty girls fitted in with everyone. Sporty girls walked tall, and you just had to respect girls who could smash it at games. I was not a sporty girl, but I wasn't like Matilda, who took almost fifteen minutes to run a mile. Soreya was quite sporty, but she didn't hang out with that lot either.

The Princess girls were the dance fanatics who fussed about with their hair at break and talked about dieting a lot. They were friendly, I got on with them, but there's no way they'd ever let Soreya and Matilda into their group, and there was no way I would ever ditch Soreya and Matilda for them.

The other group of girls in my year were the Swots, but we called them the Charlottes. Only one of them was called Charlotte – Maisie's best mate. But Soreya, Matilda and I joked that they were all so interchangeable that in our minds, the group became known as the Charlottes. These were the ones *definitely* going to university. Most of them came from families where their parents were posh and rich. They didn't live on estates – they lived in nice houses or flats and had hot dinners every night. Not Doritos and dips like we did at Nan's sometimes.

Soreya and Matilda knew my dad was dead. I told them the story about him having had a heart attack, and felt a bit bad when they were so nice about it. I wish I'd told them the truth. I really wish I had. Because somehow, a few weeks after we moved, some weird local blogger found out where we were. We found him taking photos outside Nan's flat one night, and he snapped Mum on her way home from work.

We couldn't stop him putting it on his stupid website, but he didn't exactly have a massive following, thank god. But the picture he took was clearly of Mum. He'd even found out that we'd changed our name from Lyons to Hamilton. *New Identity For Balcony Death Suspect* said the header on his blog post. Like he had a right to tell everyone who we were.

'Isn't it illegal, Mum?' Even though she'd insisted nobody would see it, I was still fighting not to get upset as we read the post.

Mum was just as upset as I was but trying not to show it. 'It's only illegal if the police give you a new identity, not your nan.'

Later that day, when I got home from popping out to get some milk, all hell broke loose.

'You what?' Mum was shouting, her face purple with rage. 'Swear to me, Jean. Swear you didn't speak to anyone about us? You did, didn't you? A glass of wine and you'll roll over and tell anyone about us!'

'I didn't!' Auntie Jean screeched back at her.

'Liar!'

'Mum! Stop it!' I shouted. She'd got hold of Jean's hair.

'I don't believe you. You told that sodding blogger about us, didn't you? How could you? Don't you get how dangerous that is?'

Jade and Becca flew in, and Becca managed to get Mum off Auntie Jean. Jade grabbed Mum's wrists and pulled her away.

'Let go of her!' I put my arm around Mum, who was crying, finally giving up the fight.

Jade was the one snarling now. 'You TOUCH my mum again, Mary . . .'

'Jade, it's all right.' Becca was calmer. 'Emma, get your mum out of here. Everyone just cool off, all right?'

They shut themselves in the kitchen while I took Mum to the front room and got her to sit down on the sofa. She was still shaking. Through the door, we could hear Jade growling, 'I swear, Mum, if she touches you again I'm gonna thrash her. I don't care, I will.'

'Auntie Jean wouldn't tell anyone about us, would she?' I asked, cuddling Mum tight. 'She wouldn't do that to us?'

Mum gave a shaky laugh. 'I wouldn't put it past her. A little bit of attention and she's anyone's, flapping her gums. She's been whingeing about not having enough room here now. We need to get out of here, get our own place. I can't stand it any more.'

'But where would we go? We can't afford anywhere, Mum.'

'I know, darling, I know. I just don't know what to do.' I held her while she cradled her head in her hands.

Later on, when Mum and Jean had both calmed down, Jade found me in the kitchen while I was making Mum a cup of tea.

'It wasn't my mum, all right?' she said.

Jade hardly ever spoke to me. I hardly saw her, to be fair. She was always out, often all night.

'How do you know?' I asked.

'I just know. So tell Auntie Mary to chill.'

Either way, Mum and I knew that when it came down to it, we only really had each other. There was no one else we could properly trust.

TEN

It wasn't long before the news of who I really was hit school.

Soreya texted me one morning with a screenshot of a WhatsApp message. **Ellie posted this in a group and everyone is sending it round. I thought you said it was a heart attack???**

The screen grab showed two pictures – one of that local blog, and the other a picture of an old article from back when Dad died, with a picture of me and my mum. Ellie had written, **She thinks she's better than everyone but her mum was up for murder?!**

Meet me at the science block. Matilda too, I replied to Soreya.

Would they still want to know me now? Would they be angry that I'd lied to them?

I was relieved to see them waiting there when I got to school. I'd made my way to the science block, avoiding eye contact with anyone in the corridors or hanging about by the school gates. 'He didn't have a heart attack,' I blurted as soon as I walked up to Soreya and Matilda. There was no point not being honest. 'I'm sorry, but I just said that because I didn't want all the trouble we had before, where I used to live. Everyone judging us, people gossiping and being horrible to Mum. That's why we left my old estate and came here.'

'Shit, that's heavy,' Soreya said.

'I get why you lied,' Matilda said. 'Everyone's got a past. No one wants their life to be exposed like that. You don't have any reason to say sorry.'

Soreya nodded in agreement. In that moment, I just loved them both.

'So . . . did you see it happen?' Matilda asked softly.

I shook my head.

'Do you think your mum did it?'

'Matilda!' Soreya said. 'That's too personal!' Then she looked at me. 'Did she, though?'

'The court didn't have enough evidence to find her guilty,' I said.

'And that's your story and you're sticking to it. Loyalty. I like it.' Matilda grinned, and I felt relieved that we were kind of joking about it all, that things were normal. I didn't want to sink again.

As I walked back in to school, I decided I should hold my head up, like Mum had said to do. After speaking to Soreya and Matilda, it felt easier to look people in the eye. They actually didn't look back, or did for just a sec before their eyes flitted away. There was no banter from the boys, not even the ones that usually tried to get my attention. They were quiet and looked away too.

Of course, the one person who wasn't quiet was Ellie.

'Watch out, here comes the murderer's daughter.'

She was early for class once, there before the teacher and obviously waiting for me.

'You don't know what you're talking about. My mum wasn't charged,' I told Ellie in front of everyone. What I had sussed, correctly, was that Ellie wasn't 'popular' as such; people were just scared of her.

'She got away with it.' Ellie smirked. 'It's obvious she did it.'

'And what do you care? Hey Ellie, why don't we talk about *your* dad for a change?'

Ellie's dad was a sore point. I'd heard he was in prison, and everybody knew you did not bring this up with Ellie. Realising that she could do no worse to me than I had been through already was freedom. I could handle her. No one had ever dared mention him to her face. I stared her down.

'At least he ain't a murderer,' she said finally.

'What's he in prison for, then?'

Suddenly Ellie's eyes were full of tears. 'Don't talk about my dad.'

Yolande, one of the Sporty girls who never usually got involved with anyone's drama, suddenly piped up. 'Oh, she can dish it but she can't take it. Bit of a useless school bully, aren't you? We're going to give the job to someone else.'

Ellie was shocked – not as shocked as me – that Yolande had got involved. Ellie wouldn't start on Yolande. She was one of those girls that you just didn't do that to. So Ellie looked at me like she wanted to kill me, but she did nothing.

After that, everyone went back to their desks, slightly disappointed, and Yolande went back to being the sports star who kept her distance. But at least it sorted Ellie out.

*

Within a few weeks at Lammas High, I was friendly with more people. Drama club was after school and free, and one hundred per cent the most fun thing at school – other than our proper Drama lessons, but they were all focused on the exams now.

Mrs Delerosh, the drama teacher, was Polish. 'My name is Delerosh, I swim in orange squash!' she sang out in my first class so I'd remember her name. Mrs Delerosh, who swam in orange squash, never seemed to worry about sounding uncool. I loved her for that. She had long hair way past her bum and wore mad jewellery: really dangly earrings, massive chunky necklaces and loads of bangles and rings that jangled when she stomped around the classroom in her purple Doc Martens boots. She spoke loudly and *always* dramatically.

'Emma darling, you are a revelation!' she said after I had learned this whole speech by Hamlet's girlfriend, Ophelia. I'd rehearsed so much at home I'd driven Nan mad.

'You are wild! Untamed! You are pure theatre without even trying! Wonderful to see, so wonderful!' Then she swept on to the next exercise.

I hung around sometimes after Drama club and helped Mrs Delerosh clear up. The other kids usually rushed off home for their dinner, but I knew Mum wouldn't be home till after her last evening cleaning job, and I didn't like hanging around Nan's flat when she wasn't there.

I chatted to Mrs Delerosh about stuff – about my mum and my nan, and where we lived, how I didn't have a bedroom of my own.

'Ah, Emma!' she said. 'Patience. We are all born in a circumstance we did not choose, but we can change our circumstances if we want to. Look at me. I was a young girl in Poland, dreaming of being a Hollywood star. I worked hard, and now here I am! Teaching Drama at an inner-city school.' She chuckled to herself. 'One day, Emma, you will have everything. I promise you. Know your own value. I can see you in costume dramas, in comedies! You have something better than beauty – you have *talent*. Such a skilled actress and performer. Now, go. Go away and I can have my cigarette in peace. I'm not allowed to smoke here, so I don't want any witnesses.'

My heart literally danced when she said I was talented. I made Soreya and Matilda laugh when I acted things out and did impressions. I did the Charlottes. *'I think poor people are so interesting. Don't you find them interesting? I'm thinking of buying one or two, just as pets.'* Even the Charlottes laughed when I did this. They all came to Drama club too.

I used Mrs Delerosh as inspiration. Her Polish accent was subtle, and I got it perfectly. *'You know, my darlings, it is not very easy being me, because I have to deal with you. No no no no!'* I'd wave my hands dramatically like she did. *'I'm not saying you are not perfect, you are, you are! I just need you to be, how do you say? Totally different.'*

She loved me doing that. 'Inhabiting other characters like that is a rare, god-given thing, Emma,' Mrs Delerosh said. 'You can't learn it. It's a gift. And don't you dare be anything different to exactly who you are.'

'You are so good at acting,' Charlotte Galbraith, the main Charlotte, said to me after the club one day, squeezing my arm. 'You're really talented, and totally teacher's pet. If I didn't like you, I'd be so jealous. *Ciao!'* And off she went with her little group, both of us knowing that at school she'd never have spoken to me.

I knew the Charlottes wouldn't want me in their world when they left school. But I didn't want to stay where people expected me to stay, do something they expected someone like me to do. I was sleeping on a roll-up mattress on the floor in my nan's house, and I sure as hell knew I didn't want to stay there for ever.

Mrs Delerosh had said we could change our own circumstances. I knew I had to change mine.

ELEVEN

One morning after Maths, a boy called Mo came up to me. 'We're going to the Bunny Park for lunch if you wanna come?'

Mo was one of the really good-looking guys in my year, but he was a shy one, not big-headed. The Bunny Park was where the popular kids hung out: the Charlottes, and the hot sporty guys like Mo. Soreya and Matilda took the piss out of the kids who went there.

I'm not sure why, but I decided I'd go with him. I didn't meet Soreya and Matilda in the canteen like usually. I chatted to Mo instead, guiltily ignoring Soreya's text. We didn't talk about anything deep, just 'what music do you like' type stuff.

I could tell that the Charlottes were trying not to look surprised when Mo came into the park with me. We'd got some chips on the way. Someone like me, who talked like me, from a family like mine, was not the the kind of company the Charlottes usually kept, but here I was, sharing chips with the hottest guy in school. I didn't care what the Charlottes thought about me being there. I just concentrated on Mo. We ate the chips and chatted, and up close I could see just how beautiful and dark his eyes were, just how long his lashes were. Having his attention felt different to some of the other boys who tried to chat to me.

'Don't go all swotty and start hanging around with the Charlottes,' Soreya told me when I got back.

I felt a bit guilty. 'I never. I just went with Mo 'cos he asked.'

'Mo's a swot,' Soreya said.

'He's a fit swot,' I told her, grinning.

'He's a boy Charlotte, though,' Matilda chimed in.

I laughed. 'Actual Charlotte was all right. She's not a cow, you know. I do Drama club with her. She can be a laugh occasionally.'

Matilda pretended to faint and clutched Soreya. 'Oh my god, it's happening, they've got her! The zombie Charlottes have got her!'

After that day at lunch, Mo started to sit next to me in class. He'd hover for a moment to check where I was going to sit, then he'd join me.

'Did you see Charlotte's face when Mo didn't sit next to her in Maths like normal?' Matilda asked me as we headed away from the gates after school. I could tell she was loving this tiny bit of drama. Mo wasn't Charlotte's boyfriend, but even so – I'd changed things. And I had seen Charlotte's face. She definitely didn't like it.

I didn't want Soreya or Matilda to know this, but I saw the benefit of being friends with the Charlottes. They had everything; they were going places. They'd shut me out so far, but now I had an opportunity to get properly in with them, and I didn't want to blow it. They shut Soreya and Matilda out too, but they didn't care and sort of accepted it. Soreya and Matilda 'knew their place', as Nan often said. But who said what your 'place' should be? What if I wanted a different place?

Thing was, could I ever be like the Charlottes with my cheap hair clips, old broken-screen phone and mat on the floor for a bed? Their clothes were always ironed and clean, their voices so confident when they spoke to a teacher, and so the teachers treated them differently. It was subtle, but they did. They understood each other, cut from the same cloth.

'Did you do this all yourself, Emma?' Mr Levison, the English teacher, had said to me when he gave my first bit of homework back. He'd hovered over my desk holding my essay on *An Inspector Calls*. Everyone had looked at me like they were sure I'd cheated.

'Yes, sir,' I'd told him, frowning slightly. Mr Levison had raised his eyebrow and put the essay on my desk without another word. He'd given me an A. But it didn't matter that I did as well as the Charlottes in lessons. It wasn't enough.

I started to change how I talked. Not massively, not fake. I just made sure to pronounce all my haitches and tees, and I spoke slower and tried to sound less rough. I wasn't trying to be something unreal, I was just . . . trying not to be stuck in the same place for the rest of my life.

Nan began to notice. 'You've started getting posh at your new school, eh? As long as you don't get ideas above your station.'

I folded my arms. 'Why do I have to have a low station, Nan?'

Mum, who usually let Nan say whatever she wanted, said, 'If she wants to better herself, that's a good thing.'

'Better than us, you mean? Charming!'

'Oh, you know I don't mean that, Mum.'

But Nan had that look on her face that she got just before she tore someone to shreds. She pointed at Mum. '*You* had the world at your feet. You were a good-looking girl, but you didn't listen to me and married that thug! Now look at you.'

Mum stopped peeling potatoes and looked angry. For a moment I thought she was going to shout at her. Nan lit a cigarette and carried on looking at her magazine like nothing had happened. Mum's face was red and I could see she was trying to stare away tears. She looked down and carried on with the potatoes.

Nan flicked her ash in a saucer. 'Look, I don't have a problem with anyone bettering themselves. I'm just saying you don't wanna be talking like you've got a poker up your bum.'

'Grandmother,' I said to Nan in an ultra-posh voice, like someone in the royal family. 'I do not talk as though I have a poker up my bottom. *This* is talking like I have a poker up my bottom. I am merely pronouncing my tees and my haitches as they are meant to be pronounced.'

Nan laughed. 'Cheeky mare. She'll be on telly one day, Mary. She'll be one of them luvvies.'

*

At school the next day, the careers advisor, Julie, came in, and we all had to talk to her about what we wanted to do. She looked at what the teachers had said about me.

'You're fairly new here I see, Emma. Your marks are good. Do you like children?'

It seemed an odd question, but I told her, yes, I did, especially little ones.

'Well, that's great,' said Julie. 'Because you're a good all-rounder for teaching in a primary school. Is that a job that would interest you?'

I did like kids, but I didn't want to work in a school. I wanted to get out of school for ever.

'Not really, miss,' I said.

'Then what do you think you might want to do?'

'Well, miss, I want to act,' I said hopefully. 'Mrs Delerosh says I'm good, and I've been writing stuff for Drama club.'

She gave me a smile like I was a kid who'd just told her they wanted to be a mermaid. 'It's nice to have a dream, isn't it?' she said. 'But that's not always going to be a realistic option. You'll need to think of a good, stable job choice. It's tough out there. You're doing well, but frankly, Emma, you're hardly Oxford University material.'

I said, 'You're hardly career advisor material either, Julie.'

It just came out. I couldn't stop myself. After that she looked angry and told me to leave. 'I can't help pupils who don't want to help themselves.' And that was it.

The week we had to do work experience, I ended up putting stuff on shelves in a supermarket. Again. Julie hadn't helped me get something even close to what I wanted. As I lined up peanut butter and jam, I thought about Miley Cyrus. Everyone thought she'd only ever be Hannah Montana from the Disney Channel. OK, so her dad was famous and she was rich, but she was still just Hannah Montana off the Disney Channel. If you're famous because little kids like you, then the chances of you making it big as a rock star are not high. But Miley reinvented herself. She got naked in her videos, danced like she was having sex and made sure there was no way she could ever be a role model to six-year-olds again. No one can tell me she didn't plan all that. She had to kill Hannah Montana to be Miley Cyrus.

It wasn't exactly the same, but I had to kill the girl from the estate.

It was time to reinvent myself.

TWELVE

Suze went and did it.

She managed to pull together enough money to lease out a location – a tiny little café. She called it The Little Cup. It was just far enough away from Elmsworth for me and Mum to feel safe visiting her. She was still getting things up and running, and had one customer in there when we first went to visit: a serious-looking bloke in a suit tapping away at his laptop. Then again, there was only room for two tables in the whole place anyway.

'It's mostly take-aways at the moment, but you got to start small and think big!' Suze said, proudly wiping down the counter.

'You've done so well, Suze,' Mum said. She was looking at the fancy cupcakes Suze had on the counter in a little glass cabinet. Things like that really impress my mum. 'It's classy, Suze, so classy.'

Suze grinned and clapped her hands in excitement. 'I mean, look at me. I was a social worker a year ago, and now I've devoted my life to flat whites and Americanos.'

'What's the difference between a flat white and an Americano?' I asked.

'About thirty pee,' she said.

I laughed. See? Even with coffee you could tweak it so it was basically the same thing but suddenly people would pay more for it. You could reinvent anything – from coffee, to Miley, to me.

I had started wearing make-up. Not just a bit of lipstick or mascara, but proper smoky eyes and long lashes.

'You look like one of them beautiful girls in old paintings,' Mum had said when she caught me posing in the full-length mirror in Nan's bedroom.

I laughed. 'What, the creepy ones whose eyes follow you around the room? Thanks Mum!'

'No! I meant just beautiful, classy.'

At school Miss Macey did not think my tighter school shirts were 'classy', though.

'Oh dear, Emma, did your top shrink in the wash?' she said and raised an eyebrow.

'Miss, that's fat shaming,' Matilda responded, winking at me.

'I'm not fat!' I protested and bounced my exercise book playfully on Matilda's head.

'So what's happening with you and Mo?' Soreya asked me.

'Nothing,' I said.

It was true. Nothing had happened, even though I was still going to the Bunny Park for lunch with him. Not every day. Just occasionally, if he saw me at lunchtime, he'd say, 'Coming?' and I would go.

Mo sometimes rolled his sleeves up, and I'd catch myself staring at his arms in French class. They were brown and toned and quite hairy. I'd quickly look away before anyone caught me, especially him. Mo made me feel shy.

'He likes you,' Matilda said and made kissing noises in the air.

I slapped her arm to get her to stop. 'How do you know?'

Matilda fluttered her eyelashes, then put on a fake deep voice. 'Do you want to come to the Bunny Park, Emma? Can you be my partner in Science, Emma? Can I please touch your hair, Emma?'

'He never said that.'

'No, but he thinks it. Do you message when you're not at school?' Soreya asked.

I felt my skin heat up. 'We WhatsApp quite a lot.'

'Has he asked you to send a naked picture yet?' Matilda asked with a chuckle.

'Gross! No!' Mo wasn't that type. He just WhatsApped me **what are you up to?** type messages, and we sent each other funny memes and stuff, nothing really flirty. I was shy and he was shy, so it hadn't moved on from GIFs.

'Seriously, one of you has to make a move,' Soreya said. 'It's so obvious you like each other. If you're not careful you'll end up being "just friends".'

'And that would make me and Soreya very sad,' said Matilda dramatically. 'We'd have nothing to take the piss out of. Do you want me to say something to him?'

'Don't you dare!'

'Why not?' she protested. 'I'd be subtle. I'd just go up to him in the canteen in front of everyone and say "Hey Mo, Emma wants to marry you, you know!"'

Usually, if Mo came up to me in the yard, Soreya and Matilda would shuffle away, making everything *so* obvious. But the next lunchtime, when he came over to talk to me, Matilda literally went, 'OK so we're just gonna stand over there for a while, guys, no biggie. Shout if you need anything!'

'Yeah, the weather's better over here, Matilda,' Soreya agreed.

'Nah, it's definitely hotter where Emma's standing!'

Then they cackled loudly. Poor Mo.

'Sorry about them. Matilda's a funny one,' I said.

Mo scoffed. 'She *thinks* she's funny.'

'Oi, she's my friend!' I jokingly shoved his arm.

He leaned towards me. 'I know, but you're so different to them. Well, actually, you're so different to everybody.'

My face burned. That was definitely something you say to someone you like, wasn't it? 'Am I?' I managed, after a few seconds. 'How am I different?'

'Oh, you're begging it now.' He smiled. 'You're different because you're not full of bullshit. You're real. You don't seem to care what other people think about you. You're your own person, y'know?'

I laughed. '"You don't care what people think about you." Now to me that sounds like you're saying "everyone thinks you're awful, but you don't mind".'

He cracked up. 'No no no, that's not what I'm saying!'

'Nah nah nah, but that's what I'm hearing,' I teased.

Then he went serious. 'You're also different because . . . you're the most beautiful girl in this whole school.' He caught my hand and held it for a moment. Right there in the yard! I didn't know what to say. I just smiled, praying I had nothing between my teeth.

Then his mates came along, and he let go of my hand. 'See you later, yeah?' He leaned towards me a bit. 'I *really* want to see you later.'

Then off he went. Leaving me just standing there with my heart pounding so hard it was practically bursting out of my school blouse.

*

I wasn't at school when Ellie started a fight with Soreya.

I'd been off helping Mum. She'd got a good cleaning job – some new tenants were moving into a big house nearby, and the place needed to be cleaned from top to bottom all in one day, ready for them. Mum had taken the job, but couldn't do it by herself, and she didn't want to share the money with Auntie Jean or Nan, so she called the school to say I was sick and had me help her.

We did this sometimes when Mum got a tenancy clean or a spring clean. Miss Macey didn't say much when I was off school. She had kids in the class who skived loads more than I did.

So when Matilda called me after school sounding really upset, I was shocked.

'Ellie went for her, you know, just flew at her. Soreya had done nothing. *Nothing*, Emma! Bust up her nose, man. I tried to get her off, but she was like a dog.'

I couldn't believe what I was hearing. Soreya was sweet, not the sort to end up in a fight. 'God, I wish I had been there. No way would I have let that happen!' I said. Ellie, of course, knew that.

'She was saying all this stuff about you. Saying you were a slag, saying you were two-faced. Eventually Soreya just told her to shut up – then bam! Ellie smacked her. Her nose is really busted up, Em!'

Soreya didn't pick up her phone. I tried three times.

'Mum, can I go?' I asked, taking off my rubber gloves and straightening up from where I'd been cleaning the skirting board in the hallway outside the bathroom.

'We haven't finished!' she said, scrubbing away at the toilet.

'Yeah, but it's my mate, she got hurt . . . Please, Mum.'

'Oh Emma, do you have to get involved?'

I was nearly crying. I couldn't lose another friend, not after what had happened with Deana. What if Matilda and Soreya both stopped talking to me? 'You don't understand, she got beaten up because of me.'

Mum sighed. 'OK. Go. There's not much left to do anyway.'

I went straight to Soreya's, where her dad opened the door. I hadn't met him before. He was tall, dark skinned and thin, with a big beard.

'Hi,' I said. 'I'm Soreya's friend Emma. Is she in please? Can I see her?'

'She's upstairs,' he said. 'A bit worse for wear. I'll bring you both up some biscuits.' He had a bit of an accent. Soreya's mum was a nurse and worked long hours, so a lot of the time it was just her and her dad in the house.

I'd never been to Soreya's before. We sometimes went to Matilda's after school. She lived in a flat on the Devonshire estate, which was nicer than Nan's. New build. She had four brothers and sisters and her mum had a thick Northern accent because she was from Leeds. She smiled a lot and brought us heaps of snacks all the time. I actually loved going there – sometimes I'd sneak an extra packet of crisps into my bag to enjoy at home.

Soreya's lip was swollen and her nose had some tape on it. The blood had been cleaned up but it was still a bit red.

'Oh no!' I gasped. 'This is so bad! I'm so sorry!'

'It's not your fault.'

I sat down on her bed. 'Did you have to have stitches?'

She shook her head. 'No. My mum said I don't need them.'

'Matilda said you were sticking up for me. You hero! I'm so sorry. I feel so bad.'

Soreya rolled her eyes. 'Ellie was getting on my nerves. I ignore her normally, but it was too much, like she was just dying to start something.'

I took Soreya's hand. 'You should have just ignored her. I don't care if that idiot calls me a slag.'

'I know, but the words just came out of my mouth. I just went "shut up" or something. I wouldn't have done if I knew she'd hit me, to be fair!' She smiled, then winced.

There was a desk in her room, and Chelsea posters on her walls. And a little bookcase with picture frames on it.

'Oh my god, is that your mum?' I picked up a picture of a really pretty woman with her hands on her hips, smiling in a nurse's uniform, her hair tied up in a headscarf.

'Yeah.'

'She's gorgeous.'

Soreya laughed. 'Yeah, I know, and I look like my dad.'

'Especially your beard,' I agreed.

'Oh, don't make me laugh, it hurts my lip.'

'Sorry,' I looked at the picture again. 'Nah. You look like your mum. Same eyes.'

She fished out a box of Maltesers and we sat eating them. I wanted to know if it was hard having her mum away at work a lot, but it felt awkward to bring up, so I just put the picture back.

'Man, that Ellie really hates you,' Soreya said.

I nodded. 'She hates everyone.'

'No, she *especially* hates you. She was so angry I stuck up for you.'

'She gonna get expelled, you reckon?'

Soreya shrugged. 'Hopefully.'

*

Ellie wasn't expelled, just suspended. Soreya got a warning too, because apparently sticking up for your mates is against school rules. I didn't want trouble. I hadn't even been at school that day, but somehow there I still was, stuck right in the middle of a fight.

'That's out of order!'

Matilda was fuming about Soreya's warning. So was I.

Soreya shrugged. 'Mrs Sharma said, "It takes two to tango."'

'Imagine if someone called Miss Sharma a slag. I bet she'd tango,' Matilda muttered.

THIRTEEN

A week or so later, I needed a new exercise book, so Mr Levison told me to go and get one from the stationery cupboard.

'You may need a hand from someone who knows the way. Any volunteers?' Mr Levison said.

Mo's hand shot up. I felt a whoosh of excitement. Maisie looked at Charlotte and made a fingers-down-her-throat gesture behind Mr Levison's back.

Mo and I were quiet on the way to the stationery cupboard, which was on the other side of the school. He'd been sending me messages with hearts and kisses after what he'd said in the yard, and he reached over to hold my hand as we walked. I looked up at him and smiled.

I was conscious of every step I was taking beside Mo, of my breathing, of my heart beating.

We stood close together when we reached the tiny stationery room. It was more of a cupboard really. A big cupboard. We were pretending to look for the right exercise book, but then I felt his fingers touch mine. It felt like my whole body was being touched. I turned towards him and looked up. He stepped forward so we were pressed against each other. He stroked my hair, then leaned down and gently kissed me.

I kissed him back.

I wrapped my arms around his neck, pulled him close. He got more heated, kissing me harder, his hands all in my hair. He pulled my shirt out from where it was tucked in my skirt and then his hand was on my skin. Big hands creeping up my stomach and on to my breasts over my bra.

'Someone might come,' I whispered.

'I don't care,' he mumbled, and put my hand on his crotch. He moaned quite loudly as I felt him underneath his trousers. 'Oh my god, you are so sexy.'

I was just saying, 'So are you,' when Mr Macadam's voice joined in with, 'Just *what* is going on here?'

We leaped off each other. I quickly tucked my shirt back in, and Mo started jabbering. 'We were just getting books, sir, and some pens . . .'

For a second I thought he'd said 'penis'. *Pens.* He said pens. At least Mo was saying something. I literally couldn't speak. I was *so* embarrassed.

'This is an educational establishment, not a brothel. Come with me, both of you.'

And he marched us to the head teacher's office for a proper telling-off. Of course, then my form teacher had to be told, and so in a flash, everyone heard that Mo and I had made out in the stationery cupboard. That meant it was no secret any more, even for people like Charlotte who'd been trying to ignore it. Mo and I were an item. I was so happy. This was more like it!

Every lunchtime we went to the Bunny Park and just made out. I didn't care who saw or who knew. All I could think about was his shoulders and his lips. I loved his shoulders – they were like a proper man's. We weren't allowed to kiss like that at school, obviously, but I sat next to him in every class we had together, and Mo would put his hand on my knee under the table and leave it there until I thought I'd actually faint.

'Oi! Get a room!' boys would sometimes call out if they saw us having a hug between classes, and Mo would whisper, 'Ignore them. They're just jealous', in my ear and make me melt.

Then, after tutorial, Miss Macey decided she needed to have a word with me.

'It's a wonderful thing when you first fall in love,' she began.

I nearly died. Who wants their teacher to talk to them about that kind of stuff? 'Oh miss, is it that obvious?' I mumbled.

'It's hardly a secret, Emma! Just try to keep your canoodling to a minimum in school, OK?'

Only Miss Macey would use a word like 'canoodling'.

'What did Miss Macey want?' Soreya asked when I went to find her and Matilda after school. Mo had a football match.

'I think she was trying to tell me not to have sex on the school property.'

'Oh my god, are you sleeping with him?' Soreya asked.

'No!' I said quickly, then added, 'Anyway, that's none of your business.'

'See, Matilda,' Soreya said, shaking her head. 'She's changed. She used to tell us everything.' She sighed dramatically. 'But now she has let a guy come before her friends.'

'Ah, no I haven't, don't say that.'

'Well, we don't see you much any more. Matilda doesn't want to admit it, but she misses you.'

Matilda pulled a face. 'No, I don't!'

I wrapped my arms around her. 'Aw, mate, I love you, too.'

Soreya flung herself on to us. 'I love you three!'

Matilda, who was not a huggy person – which was why it was funny – flapped her arms up in the air. 'All right, all right, weirdos, get off me.'

They were right, though. I'd been so wrapped up with kissing Mo whenever I could, I hadn't seen my friends enough.

'Swear you'll unglue yourself from that boy's lips more often and hang out with your true friends?' Matilda said eventually, looking really serious.

'I promise,' I said with equally ridiculous seriousness.

'Good.' She smirked a bit. 'You may now hug me one more time.'

*

It was a couple of weeks later, just before we broke up for Christmas, when Mo and I went to his house after school. He told me that his mum and dad weren't going to be home from work till six.

'You'll have to be gone by then. Is that OK?' he said. 'I don't like my mum and dad knowing my business.'

'Am I your business then?' I said, smiling at him.

He kissed me. 'Yeah, you know you're my business.'

He took my hand and led me upstairs to his room. His bedroom was small and covered in football posters. We sat down on his bed and started kissing. He put his hand under my school shirt and felt my boobs over my bra, kissing my neck and making me so hot I thought I'd scream.

'I don't want to make you do anything you don't want to do,' he whispered, stopping his kisses for a moment.

I'd thought about it. I was sixteen. Loads of girls at Elmsworth had lost their virginities before they were sixteen. I didn't want to wait any more with Mo. I really liked him. He was nice to me, he was so gentle, and he actually seemed proud to be seen with me around school.

He was the one, right? I thought as he slid his hands inside my school trousers and started touching me. I unzipped my fly and let him take them off.

I didn't tell him it was my first time. He was gentle, like I thought he would be – it only hurt a little bit. It was quick too. He finished, and then lay on top of me breathing hard. I wrapped my arms around him, but after just a moment, he reached for his phone.

'Shit. It's quarter to six. You've got to get out.'

He was really stressed. I got up, and that's when we both saw the blood on his sheets.

'Shit!'

'Erm . . .' I began.

'You didn't say you were a virgin!'

'I'm sorry!'

He yanked his sheet off and ran out of the room. I dressed quickly, suddenly feeling a bit sore and awkward when I put my underwear and trousers back on. I could hear him downstairs, obviously putting on the washing machine. I went to the bathroom to sort myself out a bit, and he was back in a flash.

'Come on, Emma, you really need to hurry. I'm so sorry, babe.'

I was quick, but the second I unlocked the door, he came into the bathroom like a sniffer dog, checking to see if I'd left any traces. He didn't kiss me again, even though I wanted him to.

I could feel his relief once we were outside and on our

way to the bus stop. 'I'm sorry, Emma, I was freaking out about my parents getting back. I want a chance to tell them about you before they meet you.'

'It's all right,' I said, looking at the pavement as I walked beside him. 'I get it.'

I wanted to be casual, but I felt like what we had done was a big deal. I'd wanted him to hold me for longer in bed. I'd wanted him to kiss me and tell me I was beautiful, not run around like a madman and pretty much boot me out of his house.

'You on the pill?' he asked me suddenly as we waited awkwardly for my bus.

My jaw clenched a bit. We hadn't used a condom. 'No.'

'Shit,' he said, running his hand through his hair. 'Can you get the morning-after pill?'

'I suppose,' I said.

All his warmth towards me had gone. I moved a bit closer to him, hoping he'd hold my hand or put an arm around me, but he didn't. 'Here's your bus!' he said with relief he couldn't hide.

*

When I walked into Nan's flat, I thought Mum would know. I felt like it was written on my face. *Ladies and gentleman! Emma has had sex!*

Of course, she didn't. But she knew there was *something* wrong.

'Is it a boy, Emma?' she said that night as we were sorting

out our beds. 'I thought you'd been seeing someone. You've been extra bouncy lately. But now you're down. I know the signs. What is it?'

It was a relief to have an excuse to tell her about Mo. I hadn't told her before because it felt special having a nice secret for a change. But now it didn't feel so nice any more.

'Well, who is he? From your school?'

I reassured her he was cool and not a thug. Mum was always worried I'd end up with a thug.

'Have you had sex with him?'

I couldn't believe she was already straight out asking me that. 'Mum!'

'It's OK if you did. You are legal, you know. Just be careful. Don't make the same mistakes I did.'

I felt my heart judder, remembering Mo asking me to get the morning-after pill. 'Do you regret having me or something?'

She rolled her eyes. 'I just mean that it was hard, and I want you to have an easier life than I had.' Then she added, 'Than I'm *having*, to be perfectly honest . . .'

We got into our beds and I pulled the blanket around me tightly, thinking.

*

Mo didn't text me that night, but he came to find me in the yard at school the next day.

'You OK?' he asked casually.

I told him I was. I was so glad that he wasn't the type to go blabbing to his mates . . . Except it turned out he had.

The minute I walked into Drama club, Charlotte pulled me aside. 'Look, I can't pretend I don't know what happened, Emma. Mo's a mate, and he needed someone to talk to.'

I really hadn't wanted Mo to talk to anyone but me about what we did. I couldn't believe he'd gone running straight to Charlotte.

'He's freaking out that you didn't use a condom,' she was saying. 'You can't blame him.'

My mouth went dry. Oh god, I didn't need more gossip. 'Charlotte, this is none of your business. It's fine and it's between me and Mo,' I said, as coolly as I could.

'Oh, I know,' she said, tossing her hair. 'I completely get it. I won't tell a soul.'

That afternoon after school, Mo didn't call me or arrange to meet me. He was ignoring my texts, and he didn't sit next to me in class at all. People were starting to notice.

I was confused. What had happened?

I knew Charlotte had told Maisie and her other friends about me and Mo. I'd secretly hoped Charlotte and I would end up being friends, but that clearly wasn't going to happen. She loved knowing that I'd slept with Mo, and even more that he regretted it.

Soreya and I went to Matilda's house after school. I was in a state. Mo had completely ignored me all day.

'It's rank what he's doing,' Matilda said, shaking her head.

Soreya nodded fiercely. I loved her for being there for me, even though what I did was something she would never ever do. She wasn't going to have sex with anyone until she was married, she'd said.

Matilda carried on, 'Like, you wouldn't have slept with him if you'd known he was gonna ghost you after. Guys should be upfront about whether or not they are dickheads before they have sex with you. Give you a clearer idea of whether or not they're gonna make you feel like shit.'

I mimicked Charlotte. 'Mo needed someone to talk to.' I shook my head, fuming. One thing I knew for sure: I wouldn't be talking to *him* any more.

FOURTEEN

'So did you get a morning-after pill in the end?' Matilda asked. 'You can get them from the clinic for free, you know. My cousin works in a chemist and she said they're like twenty quid from there!'

I nodded. I knew all about the free pill. Mum had got me one the moment I'd told her we hadn't used a condom. She'd had to pretend it was for her when she went to the clinic, because she didn't like the idea of how it might look if I went to get one myself. Definitely not 'classy'.

Soreya and Matilda didn't think I should text Mo again.

'But why play games?' I said with frustration. 'We had sex. *Sex!* Why should I suddenly play it cool when he's trying to act like none of it happened?'

'Just ignore him and he'll come running,' Soreya said. 'Trust me. I have zero experience with boys, but I watch a *lot* of TV.'

'I don't see why I should have to trick him into getting in touch,' I protested. But maybe she was right.

Mo eventually texted me back; but just the once, saying, **Sorry, I'm so deep in revision. I'll call when I come up for air.** He had to have suffocated, because a couple of days went by and still nothing. Then a few days later at lunch, I heard:

'Oi! Tramp. How's your psycho mum?'

Ellie was back from her suspension.

'And I heard you really are a slag, too,' she went on. 'A slag that's just been *dumped*!'

Brilliant. Seemed Ellie knew more about what was going on with Mo than I did. She wouldn't try anything in the dinner hall with teachers all milling about, but she couldn't help kicking me when I was down. I forced myself to be calm, to breathe.

'If you think being vile to me is going to make you feel any better about yourself, then you've wasted your time,' I said evenly. 'Whatever happens with me and Mo, however often you call me a slag, you know you'll always be this sad loser that nobody likes.'

Ellie spat right in my face. Then she stood there, glaring, holding her dinner tray. I didn't hang around. Instead, I wiped my cheek and went to find Mo. I didn't care what they did on TV shows. This was my real life.

He was standing with some mates in the yard. I went right up to him.

'Can I speak to you, Mo?'

He looked embarrassed. 'Sure.'

We walked to a quiet part of the yard, by the sports field. The second I started talking, my voice cracked like I was gonna cry. 'What have you said about me to people? Why do people think you've dumped me?'

Mo looked at me. 'Ah, Emma, I never said anything to anyone.'

I folded my arms to stop my hands trembling. 'What about Charlotte, then? How did she know what had happened?'

He sighed. 'I just put a few people straight who asked, that's all. And I haven't "dumped" you.'

'Well, you haven't called me back or wanted to see me since I came to your house.'

Mo looked really uncomfortable. 'Look, I mean I haven't dumped you because we weren't really *going out*. Not properly. It just didn't feel one hundred per cent right. You know?'

That was all it took. The tears spilled out of my eyes and I was really crying. Soreya and Matilda spotted me from across the yard and I saw them coming over.

'It would really have been nice to know that before we had sex, *you know*?' I said to Mo sarcastically, mimicking him through my tears.

'I know Emma, I'm so sorry . . .'

Soreya was suddenly by my side. 'What have you said to her?' she snarled at Mo. 'Why have you upset her?'

Mo put his hands up defensively and backed away, saying, 'I'm sorry', one more time. I barely heard it. I turned and cried on Soreya's shoulder, right there where everyone could see.

Soreya patted me on the back. 'Matilda,' she said, 'you got any Skittles left?'

'Yeah.'

'Good. Now feed them to Emma. It's an emergency.'

I laughed and cried at the same time as Matilda carefully posted Skittles into my mouth over Soreya's shoulder.

'Focus on the Skittles, Emma, forget about the boy,' Soreya said soothingly. 'Just think about the sweets.'

Eventually, I straightened up and wiped my face on my shirt sleeve. 'We had sex, I got blood on his sheets, and all I get is a pathetic "I'm sorry"?'

Soreya and Matilda screwed up their faces.

'Too much information, babe,' said Soreya. 'But yeah, he's scum. Forget about him.'

*

'Life ain't a Disney film, you know,' Nan said.

She was in the kitchen when I got home and told my mum about everything that had happened at school. About Ellie, about the spitting, about Mo. I was crying again. It felt like the tears hardly ever dried up these days. I'd been happy for a while – but like everything, it had all fallen apart again too quickly.

'Mum!' said my mum. 'Can't you see she's upset?'

'I'm just saying,' Nan protested. She was always 'just saying'.

'It's not helping.' Mum looked at me. 'Now you listen to me, Emma. This Mo didn't deserve you. He's just a stupid little boy who was very lucky to have a chance with you. He's a bullet dodged as far as I'm concerned. He isn't worth it.'

Nan nodded. 'Your mum's right, Emma. You can take your pick of blokes.' She put out her cigarette and lit another. 'You're a clever girl, and pretty. Like your mum was.'

'Thanks, Mother,' Mum said sarcastically.

'I just mean she'll have her pick of men! Don't sell yourself short, love.'

Mum pulled me to her for a hug. 'Your nan is right. You can do much better than him. He sounds so immature.'

Nan put a cup of tea in front of me. 'Boys mature much later than girls – and some of them never make it,' she chuckled.

'It's horrible though, Mum. He doesn't even say hello to me properly now,' I said, sighing into the steam of my cuppa as I took a sip. 'Like nothing happened. Like he doesn't know me.'

Mum pressed her lips together. 'He feels awkward, darling,' she said. 'I don't think he means to hurt you. He doesn't know what to say. Stay away from him. Act like you don't care.'

That seemed to be the advice from everyone. When you're really hurting, act like you are not. Lucky acting was one of the things I was actually good at.

Nan said, 'I'm more concerned about the Ellie girl. Spitting like a right thug. What are we gonna do about her?'

'"We" are doing nothing,' Mum said. 'I'm going to call the school.'

'Leave it,' I begged. 'Please. I can handle Ellie. I'm not scared of her. Please don't call the school, it'll make things worse.'

I'd wanted to hit Ellie when she'd spat at me, to tell the truth. I'd wanted to punch her lights out. I was too ashamed to tell my mum that part. I still saw the things that happened with Dad when I was little, replaying in my head. I didn't want to be like that.

I still found my mind going back to the night he fell. Me in my bedroom and Mum out there on the balcony with him, screaming and crying. *'Get off! Get off me!'* Some people who'd been drinking with him in the pub that night said in court that when he'd left he could barely walk. Then he was fighting with Mum, and – down he went. Twelve floors. I didn't see what happened, but if I was truthful, I didn't care if Mum had done it or not. I had my suspicions. But all I really knew was, like her, I'd wanted it to be over.

And then it was.

Before I got into my makeshift bed in Nan's living room that night, I washed my face twice with soap, thinking about what had happened, still feeling the slick of Ellie's saliva hitting my cheek.

I'd called Soreya earlier as I walked to the shops.

'Spitting on someone is assault, you know,' Soreya said in disgust. 'You did good, walking away.'

'I really wanted to punch her, Soreya.'

'But you didn't.'

None of the Charlottes would have thought about punching someone, even if they'd been spat at. I thought I could aim for being 'classy', like Mum was always on about, but I hadn't managed it yet.

I hated admitting this to myself, but I was more like Ellie than I was like the Charlottes. I belonged much more in her world than theirs.

FIFTEEN

At school over the next week or two, it felt like all anyone could mention when it came to me was that I'd been dumped by Mo. But at last, it was the Christmas holidays and I could get a break from school, even if it meant I didn't get to see Matilda and Soreya every day. It also wasn't much of a holiday with Mum and Auntie Jean's massive rows.

Whenever it all kicked off, Nan basically just lit a fag and made herself a cup of tea.

'They've always been like this, Emma,' she'd say to me as it unravelled around us. 'They get on for a bit, then fight like cat and dog. I just don't get involved no more. I just block it out. After a while, all their shouting sounds like the sea.'

It was hard, though, blocking out all the screaming and shouting and shoe-throwing. At least Becca and Jade didn't really bother with me. They were in their own little worlds, and went out pretty much every night. No one asked where.

I did wonder where they got their money from, though. Neither of them seemed to work.

'God knows, Emma,' Mum said when I brought it up. 'I don't think it's something we want to know.'

'There's no jobs for my girls,' Auntie Jean said when I asked *her* why they didn't work. 'They give all the jobs to the immigrants and foreigners.'

'Immigrants AND foreigners?' I repeated, smiling.

Nan was on a roll. 'Every builder you see opens their mouth and you realise it's a foreigner. Polish or whatever. Every single one.'

'Becca and Jade can't get any building work? That's sad.'

'Don't take the mick,' Auntie Jean said, frowning. 'And it's not just the builders. The new GP is a Pakistani bloke, didn't you say, Mum?'

Nan went, 'I think so. Or Indian.'

'What?' I put my hand to my chest. 'They gave the GP job to a qualified Pakistani doctor instead of to Jade?'

Nan laughed and I scarpered before the tea towel Jean threw hit me.

Becca's boyfriend was called Jimmy. She lived mostly at his place, it seemed, especially over the Christmas break, but when they came round to Nan's he never spoke. Ever. Even if you just said, 'Hiya, you all right?' he looked terrified, like you'd asked something really personal. He'd turn red and mumble something nobody could understand. I could see why they liked each other. Becca just bumbled along not doing or saying much, either.

Jade was sparkier than Becca. Every now and then, we'd have a chat or a bit of a laugh, but then the next day – or sometimes even the next minute – she was shut off again and I was invisible to her. She didn't seem to have a regular boyfriend.

On a very rare night a couple of days before Christmas, we were watching TV by the faint multi-coloured light of Nan's plastic Christmas tree while the others were all out. Jade turned to me out of the blue and said: 'What's it like being so pretty?' She said it so normally, not like a compliment, like it was an undeniable fact about me, so I couldn't do my usual, 'Oh, shut up, I'm not!'

'What do you mean, what's it like?' I asked instead.

'Fellas instantly liking you. Other girls must hate you. I know I do sometimes, when you come out of your room first thing in the morning looking all perfect, and I look like Shrek.'

I laughed. 'You don't look like Shrek! You're pretty. And anyway, it's not always the guys I like who like me back.' I tried not to think about Mo, but I got that heavy feeling in my belly.

'Blokes do like you, though,' Jade insisted. 'That's why Becca never stays round here with her man any more. She thinks he fancies you and you might steal him.'

I was about to laugh before I realised she wasn't joking. The idea that I might run off with Becca's bloke was pretty out there, but I didn't want to be rude about him to her sister.

'That's mad,' I said. 'Even if I liked him, I couldn't steal him. You can't steal people who don't want to go.'

'That's not how Becca sees it,' Jade went on. 'She's so insecure, she does everything she can from stopping him being around any other girls, let alone a girl like you.'

'Wow,' I said. 'That's full-on. Keeping her boyfriend from seeing *any* other girls? No wonder she hasn't got a job. That must take up all her time.'

Jade stifled a chuckle, and I felt pleased. I'd actually made her laugh. Perhaps my cousin might be friends with me after all.

*

Auntie Jean was so excited when her husband texted her out of the blue to say he was coming to see her and 'his girls' for Christmas. She ran about tidying everything, and she got her hair done, and got Jade to do her nails. I asked her where he went when he went away and she just said, 'Here, there and everywhere.'

He was called Bertie. The sort of name a cute old man would have – but there was nothing cute about Auntie Jean's Bertie. He was a rat-faced man, skinny but somehow with a belly that hung over his tracksuit bottoms. He smoked constantly, and looked at me in a way that made me want to hide every scrap of myself away from his eyes. He didn't say much when he turned up, and spent all his time on the sofa staring at the TV.

He stayed for Christmas Day. Just assumed he was invited. We couldn't all fit around the kitchen table so I had to have my Christmas dinner propped up on a stool by the sink. He wasn't my dad; he was Jade and Becca's. One of them should have given up their seat. I tried to focus on actually having a full plate for once, enjoying the slice of ham and ready-made oven roasties, veg and Bisto gravy.

After our Christmas dinner, Bertie gave me, Jade and Becca a quid each. A *quid*. Like we were four and wanted money for sweets. I mumbled my thanks. We each got a tenner from Nan, which really made my eyes light up, and watches in a proper gift box from the market.

Mum's present to me was the best, though. She must have saved up for ages to buy the beautiful silver statement earrings she knew I'd been drooling over in the Argos catalogue.

'Ah Mum! They were so dear!' I gasped. 'We're meant to be saving.'

'It's Christmas!' Mum said with a shrug.

Mum and Jean even managed to get through the day without killing each other, and at one point even had a laugh.

So it came as a big surprise to everyone, mostly me, when on Boxing Day Auntie Jean accused me of flirting with Bertie. She'd found pictures on his phone, of me. I was asleep in all of them, I quickly pointed out, disgusted.

Mum went absolutely mad. 'So he's been creeping into the front room and taking pictures while we were sleeping, and you have the nerve to say that's my Emma's fault? He's a perv, Jean! Why let him back in your life every time?'

Jean wasn't having that. 'You must have done *something* or said *something* to make him do it,' she spat.

'What, she flirted with him while she was in bed, sleeping?' Mum interjected.

Nan, unsurprisingly, found a way to stick up for Jean. 'Well, Emma is a pretty girl and she knows it . . .'

That again? 'Oh my god, Nan!' I said. 'Now you're gonna say it was my fault for wearing shorts and a vest in bed.'

'Well, a man's a man, my darling,' said Nan, looking away.

'I'm allowed to wear pyjamas in bed!'

This was unreal. It was seriously the last straw. I knew Mum and I needed to get out of there and fast. But how? We still had no money for a place of our own.

Over the holidays, I found a kiosk on the high street and got my phone screen fixed using the tenner Nan had given me. I looked at all those girls on Instagram, the ones who made loads of money through free stuff, sponsorships or were being given money to promote things. They all seemed to have the same hair, lip jobs, poses, pouts. Could I do that? Could I just put up a load of nice pictures of myself and get followers and money? Could it be that simple?

It was worth a try.

Mum took the first pictures, nice ones – *classy*, of course – and I started an Instagram page @emmahamilton_16. A few selfies, a few of me pouting and playing with my hair, copying what I'd seen, tagging myself with stuff like #sweetsixteen and #classicbeauty. Sure enough, after a while I started to get followers, and not just Soreya and Matilda.

Mum had a side hustle going on too. Her money didn't just come from her cleaning work. She was still all right looking, for a mum, and even though she hadn't had a proper boyfriend since Dad, she was on dating websites. She'd get dolled up on the weekends and go out to meet guys. No one regular. 'Who'd have me with my baggage?' she'd say.

'You could try death row. Those blokes aren't very picky.'

She'd slap my shoulder. 'I'll have you know I am still very much in demand. You're not the only hottie in the family.'

Some of these blokes she was meeting were clearly giving her a bit of money. But if she talked about any of them, she just called them 'my friends'. She showed me pictures of a few of these 'friends'. They were all old, balding, podgy men.

'Well, you've certainly got a type, Mum.' The type who would be grateful for having someone decent-looking like Mum on their arm. A woman they'd spend a bit of cash on.

'Looks aren't everything.'

'Says the woman who says my looks can get me everything I want!'

One of these friends seemed to stick a bit more. Thomas, who came over on Saturday mornings in his van to take Mum out for a drive. Thomas was a businessman, Mum said. I knew Thomas was a man-with-a-van removal driver. I'd seen his card in Mum's bag. But either way, he took her off for an hour before he started his Saturday jobs on the weekends, and gave her a few quid to help her out. Aunt Jean and Nan clocked that Mum was using him. Jean, surprisingly, stuck up for her. 'You got to do what you got to do in the world.'

No one thought to hide any of this from me. Whatever Mum was up to, I wasn't complaining. We were saving up to get our own place, after all. I wanted to leave school and start working, too, so we could get there faster. I could clean, work in a shop – anything to get us on our feet and out. I couldn't get out of going to school, though. Not till I'd done my GCSEs. I didn't know why I had to sit the exams. I needed to get a job now.

I tried again to apply for Saturday jobs, and to my total relief, this time I actually got one – in the café by the Bunny Park from 8am till 3pm. Mr and Mrs Jeenal who owned it were all right. They paid me out of the takings in the till at the end of each shift. It wasn't ever very much – less than Mum's cleaning – because I was only sixteen and they could get away with it. I was a bit weary of people from my school coming in – especially Mo and that lot – although they didn't tend to go there on the weekends. But going home with money in my pocket that I had made myself was the best feeling in the world. Especially when I gave every penny I made to Mum.

*

As much as I dreamed about finding a job that paid more, I couldn't avoid school. Not without attracting attention from social services, and that was the last thing Mum needed. At least I didn't have long to go. By the time we were heading for the Easter break, I felt like the end was in sight, and I was saving up money from the café as much as I could.

My mocks went all right, considering I hardly revised. But that didn't change my mind about leaving school after my GCSEs were done. My tutors in all my subjects (except for Geography, which was so boring I had no idea why I'd taken it) reckoned I was going to do well in my exams if I found 'the right focus'. They all loved to bang on about doing A-levels and stuff, but I already had 'the right focus'. I wanted to get out of there and make some money. My Instagram followers were going up by the day, and even if I wasn't making any money from that yet, I could definitely see the potential. And when I posed in my mirror in little shorts and vests, that definitely got my likes up. But still, every night, I slept on my nan's floor, next to my mum sleeping on the sofa.

There was nowhere quiet I could do my revision in Nan's flat. Teachers kept telling me I could always stay behind in the school library, but most days after school I'd been helping Mum with cleaning jobs. All I had to do was scrape by in my exams anyway, and then I was out of there.

'You two both *live* in the library now,' I moaned to Soreya and Matilda. 'You're no fun any more.'

Matilda said, 'We can't all rely on our beauty and charm to get ahead, you know, Emma. Some of us, like Soreya here, have to work really hard.'

They talked about doing their A-levels and going to uni, looking at which ones they were going to apply to when the time came.

'I'm definitely going to stay in London. My parents won't let me move out,' Soreya said. 'That's fine with me, though. My mate went to uni somewhere in the countryside, and she said, honestly, they'd never seen a brown person around there. I can't handle that!'

Matilda was the opposite. 'I want to go up north, get to know somewhere completely new.'

I got that sinking feeling, even with all my plans for earning money. My mates were heading off to have a new, exciting time and I would be left behind.

Matilda sensed my mood. 'Emma, you've got a good chance of going to uni if you want to. You just need "a tight revision schedule",' she said in her Miss Macey voice. 'No messing about.'

'Nah.' I told her, slumping down a bit in my seat. 'It's not for me.' How could I have 'a tight revision schedule' at Nan's anyway? The only time I was alone there was in the loo.

Back in January, after our mocks, Miss Macey had given me a serious talk. I'd had to go and see her in the lunch break, which I didn't exactly appreciate. She had fixed me with a look that let me know she was going in for a lecture.

'Emma, I understand things have been tough on you. I know a bit about your personal circumstances . . .' I raised an eyebrow at her, and she took a breath, then pressed on. 'And I know everything else that's been happening at school. But you have to be a fighter. You have a great deal of intelligence, Emma. If you worked hard, you could easily pass enough GCSEs to do three A-levels and apply to university.'

She might as well have told me that if I worked hard enough I could buy a magic unicorn and ride it to Tesco's. On what planet could I go to university? And with what money?

I told her what I'd told the girls. 'Miss, all that's just not for me.'

She actually sat back in surprise like I'd said the weirdest thing ever. 'Why ever not?'

Did she really not know? Did she really not realise how impossible it would be?

'I don't see the point, miss,' I said. 'Why get into debt when I could be working? It would hold me back three years at least.'

She still had that surprised look on her face, but she smiled a bit. 'Well, that's a novel way of looking at education – that it might actually hold you back.'

'I can see how you might think it sounds stupid, miss, but I don't mean it like that,' I told her. 'I mean right now, my mum and I, we need money. Right *now*, not in a few years when I've got qualifications.'

'Oh Emma, I do understand.' I still wasn't sure she really did. 'I know you are in a tricky situation. Just promise me you will think seriously about it. Don't close the door on it. Especially on drama. You're so talented, Mrs Delerosh is always telling me. Universities aren't going anywhere. Maybe in a year or two, things will be different . . .'

I have to say, she did make me think about it a bit more, especially the idea of drama school. That night when I got home, I told Mum what Miss Macey had said. She looked a bit lost, like she couldn't get her head round what I was saying. To Mum, going to university, becoming Prime Minister and owning a private island were the same thing – completely out of reach to people like us.

While that seed was sitting in my head, I had a look online, to see what was out there. There was a place that did a course after A-levels where you could actually do acting and go for castings, and even a module on stand-up comedy. For your actual *degree*.

'And then what?' I could hear my nan saying. 'Prance about for three years, go to Hollywood and marry Johnny Depp? Don't make me laugh.'

I decided to come back down to Earth and stick to a plan that was actually possible. But it was nice to dream, even if just for a moment.

SIXTEEN

A few weeks before our first proper exams, Elliot Gonzales asked me out.

Elliot was a sixth former that Soreya in particular was always drooling over. She'd make a drama out of seeing him around and clutch my arm going, 'It's him! It's Elliot. I'm going to faint! Catch me!' To be honest, everyone talked about how hot Elliot Gonzales was, so it was like Soreya saying she fancied Justin Bieber. It genuinely didn't cross my mind that she would be bothered when he asked me out.

I'd seen him looking at me when I was in the yard, and he'd come out the sixth-form block once and smiled right at me. Just smiled, with his hands in his pockets. I'd smiled back, he'd smiled again, then he went back into their separate common room.

These little meet-ups went on for a while. Then one day after school Elliot pulled up beside me in his car when he saw me walking home. The window went down and I could see him grinning at me and beckoning me over.

'Hello,' I said, grinning back.

'Hello. Emma, right?'

I nodded, even though I doubted he really didn't know my name by now.

'We could go on smiling at each other for months, or you could get in my car and I could take you for a milkshake at Iceshack,' he said.

I shrugged, trying to seem nonchalant, but I jumped into his car. Elliot was not shy. He was not shy at all. He was so different to Mo.

'You know he's been picked for the Chelsea under-eighteens team,' Soreya had told me. She and her brother were really into football. I wasn't. All it meant to me was that he was fit – and now, amazingly, he liked me.

At Iceshack, we sat in a booth and he bought us a massive chocolate ice-cream shake to share.

'So what's it like being so completely and utterly beautiful?' Elliot said as I was taking a sip.

I had to concentrate on swallowing as his eyes sparkled at me. 'What's it like being totally ripped?' I replied, smirking.

'It's a burden, let me tell you. Girls just want me for my body. I've got a mind as well, you know.'

'Yeah? So what's on your mind?'

'Right now? You,' he said, then shook his head. 'God no, that was a terrible line! Rewind, rewind!'

I shook my head, laughing. 'No rewinding! No mercy! You said it. You are cringe!'

We took the piss out of each other and laughed a lot. I enjoyed myself, and definitely decided it counted as a date.

When we were back in his car, he leaned in and kissed me clumsily. After a minute he pulled away and went serious and said, 'I need to just look at your beautiful face.' Then he kissed me properly – like so soft, so sweet. Much better.

Eventually he took me home. I couldn't really hear anything Mum or Nan or Auntie Jean said when I got in, because I couldn't stop thinking about Elliot. I floated to bed that night, closing my eyes and reliving his kisses until I fell asleep.

*

There was no way I was telling anyone about this. Not yet. Not even Soreya and Matilda. This was too huge. Elliot Gonzales, an actual sixth former, with a car and cash, was interested in me? I didn't want any chat or gossip about it. It was my beautiful secret, us seeing each other, our secret kisses . . . I couldn't blab to my mates like a little girl. I wanted him to see I was mature, someone he could trust.

Every day that next week when he didn't have football, he waited for me around the block after school and we drove to his and hung out. We didn't just kiss – we talked loads, listened to music, he heated up food his mum had made. She was from Jamaica, so I had delicious food I'd never had at Nan's house. And then we started *more* than kissing . . . but I didn't want to go all the way with him. Not even the fourth or fifth time I was there.

'Ah man!' he said, laughing as I pulled his hands away. 'It's so frustrating! You're so beautiful. I just want to be all over you.'

But I wouldn't, not after what had happened with Mo. I wanted this time to be special. If we were a bit less rushed, had a bit more time . . .

'Can I stay the night sometime?' I asked about a week later, biting my lip anxiously. I wasn't sure what he'd say.

He shook his head. 'No. My mum wouldn't like that. She's old fashioned.'

My mum wasn't old fashioned – or at least she wouldn't do much more than raise an eyebrow. But of course we had no room at Nan's.

I sighed softly. 'Have you introduced a girlfriend to her before?'

His last serious girlfriend, Katie Bell, had been a Charlotte in the year above him. I'd looked her up on Facebook. She was at Edinburgh University now, miles away. Good.

'Yeah,' he said. 'Katie came on holiday with me and my mum.'

Jealousy stabbed at my insides. I prayed it didn't show on my face. I wanted to be close to him; closer than she had been. Stupid, I know, to be jealous of a girl he went out with before he even met me.

'Can I meet your mum?' I said, trying to sound breezy, but watching him closely. 'Would she like me, do you reckon?'

'Course she'd like you. But . . . I think I still need to give her time to get over Katie. She was more upset than me when we broke up.'

That was information I didn't need. I was too jealous now to say any more without sounding crazy, so I flung myself at him and kissed him some more. Elliot was a gentleman. A truly gentle man. He didn't rush me; he didn't make me feel like I was a secret.

He did have to drive me home every time though, before his mum got home.

*

The weekends weren't really great for trying to meet up with Elliot. My job at the café took up my Saturdays, and he had training or hung out with his mates or his mum most Sundays. At school, I met up with him at lunch when he could, but he often just stayed in the sixth-form block to revise. There was no messing with him, which was a bit frustrating, but there were also no immature games – just his big beautiful smile whenever we did finally meet up.

After about a week or so, Matilda messaged me. **OK so I've got to ask . . . Are you going out with Elliot Gonzales?**

I called her straight away. 'Oh my god!' I squealed. If it was out there, then I could finally talk to her about it. 'How do you know?'

'I saw you on Bailey Street last night. My gran and auntie live at the end of that road. I saw you as I was walking back home with my dad, didn't I.'

Elliot lived on Bailey Street.

'Why didn't you say hello?' I said, feeling a bit wary. Matilda sounded flat, annoyed.

'Because you were walking along with his tongue down your throat. I was with my dad. I didn't know what to say. You didn't see me. Or maybe you did but you blanked me.'

Matilda was never angry with me, or with anyone. I wondered what I'd done wrong.

'I'd never do that!' I said.

'How do you think Soreya's going to feel?' Matilda demanded. 'Not just that you're with Elliot, but that you've kept it from her?'

Shit. I knew Soreya kind of had a crush on Elliot, but I'd never seen her get into anything serious with a boy. The last thing I wanted to do was to upset Soreya, or hurt her feelings. Soreya and Matilda had my back every time something was wrong at school. They stood up for me, made me laugh. I should have said something to them. I should have trusted them.

154

'But she doesn't really like him, does she?' I protested weakly. 'I thought that was just jokes.'

'It's not just you that has feelings for people, you know, Emma. Why would Soreya liking a guy be just "jokes"?'

I couldn't answer that without sounding like the most awful person. Because honestly? I thought it was jokes because I knew that Soreya wasn't the type of girl Elliot would go for. I assumed that she'd imagined the same.

But my silence on the phone while I tried to think of a better answer to Matilda's question made it really obvious that I thought I was hotter than my friend.

I was an arsehole.

'I'll tell her about me and Elliot,' I said quickly. 'I . . . I was stupid, I didn't think. I should have told her from the start.'

'Yeah, you should've.' I could tell Matilda was still pissed off. 'I'll see you at school,' she said, then ended the call before I could say anything else.

Soreya and Matilda were my best friends and they came as a pair. I felt sick that I'd upset them.

I needed to fix this.

*

The next morning, I texted Soreya to say I'd meet her at the corner of her road and walk to school with her. It was twenty minutes out of my way, but this was important. She never texted back, but I went anyway.

155

'I know, OK? Matilda told me,' she said as soon as I saw her. Then she took off really fast, not really walking with me.

'I'm so sorry, Soreya. I didn't know you'd be upset about me and Elliot—'

'I'm not upset,' she said, cutting me off. 'But friends tell each other stuff, Emma. They don't keep secrets. If you don't mind, I want to walk to school on my own. So can you please stop following me?'

There was no point me sticking around when she was in such a mood with me. I changed my route and went the long way round.

I found Matilda and Soreya at lunchtime.

Of course, I didn't quite kick things off in the best way. 'Why are you mad at me?' I demanded. I'd got more and more upset about it as the morning had gone on, and my question came out angry.

So Soreya got angry too. 'What makes you think I'm mad at you?'

''Cos I'm going out with Elliot.'

'I've told you what the issue is, Emma,' said Soreya. 'Come on, Matilda.'

Matilda hesitated for a second before following her. And then there I was in the middle of the yard on my own, trying not to cry.

After school, I met up with Elliot at Iceshack. Now that

most people knew we were seeing each other, it didn't seem too big a deal to do something more public.

'My mate's not talking to me because she liked you,' I told him glumly.

He grinned. 'Is she fit?'

'Be serious!'

'Well, she's not a good mate then, is she?' he said, his face a bit more serious. 'She'd be happy for you if she was.'

'It's not that simple,' I said. 'This may come as a surprise to you because I'm completely wonderful, but I don't have that many friends.'

'You don't need any now, babe. You got me.' He drained his milkshake and pecked me on the lips as he stood up. 'I gotta go, I got football. Don't let it bother you, Emma.'

But it did bother me. It bothered me a lot. Soreya was normally so chilled out and funny. This must have really mattered for her to react this way. And it mattered to me that I didn't lose my friend.

That whole next week, I was miserable about Soreya. I didn't talk to Elliot about us falling out again, though. He wasn't interested. I could tell he thought it was babyish, the idea of girls fighting – even if it was over him.

The next Sunday night, I got a text from Soreya. **Meet me before school?**

My heart leaped. Cautiously I texted back: **K.**

I met her in the café by the Bunny Park half an hour before school started. I had worked there all day on Saturday and hadn't had much time to just chill, but I was glad Soreya wanted to talk. She was already there when I arrived, with two cups of tea that she'd bought for us.

'You come to give me a hand, Emma?' Mrs Jeenal said with a chuckle.

'Just meeting my friend,' I said. I *hoped* she was still my friend, anyway.

I sat down opposite Soreya, who was not smiling. Mrs Jeenal put a currant bun in front of each of us. 'On the house,' she said with a wink.

Once Mrs Jeenal left, Soreya cleared her throat.

'I was out of order the other day,' she said flatly.

I exhaled with relief. 'It›s all right. I should've told you. It's not that I didn't want you to know, it's just that after Mo and everything, you know . . .'

'I know. Look, you've got no explaining to do, Emma. Your life is your life.' She tried for a smile, and I gratefully returned it. 'I don't want no deep and meaningful conversation, but I'm sorry, OK? Are we cool?'

In that moment I just loved her. 'We are cool,' I said, my smile widening.

'I mean, I still think you're a rubbish mate, but I guess you are entitled to a private life.' Soreya chuckled, and I flicked a currant at her. We burst into giggles. She was back – thank god. As much as I was enjoying hanging out with Elliot, I wasn't looking to lose any of my girls over a boy.

*

'It's not just about sex, you know,' Elliot told me one lunchtime around a week later, holding my hand. We were back in the café – it felt like I spent most of my life there. 'I mean, obviously I want to, but it's you. I like you. I love getting to know you.'

I sat there, stunned. Then, without warning, without giving me time to blink it away, a big fat tear fell from my eye.

'Emma?' said Elliot with concern. 'What's the matter? What did I say?'

'I'm just . . . so happy.' I laughed, wiping the tear away.

'Ah, babe!' He put his arm around me and I buried my face in his neck, breathing in his smell, crying a bit more and laughing and kissing him.

A brilliant few weeks went by. We spent lunch together every day. I even went to watch him play football.

'It was actually, like, exciting!' I told Soreya and Matilda. 'He's so fast, like a pro!'

Soreya said, 'Aw, it's so cute how proud of him you are.'

'Of course she's proud,' Matilda said with a chuckle. 'The man can kick a ball in the right direction! What girl wouldn't be proud?'

I gave her a sarcastic laugh but then reached over and squeezed Matilda into a hug, planting a big kiss on her cheek.

'Eurgh!' she said, dramatically wiping it off. 'What d'you do that for?'

I grinned. 'I just love you.'

'Well, can you not please?' she replied, pretending to be disgusted. But then she looked away and mumbled, 'I love you too.' I stared at her, open-mouthed, and she got all embarrassed. 'Shut up! I didn't say anything!'

The three of us all hugged then, before falling about into more giggles. It felt weird to say, but for once, things were actually going really well.

SEVENTEEN

Valentine's Day was on a Sunday, and Elliot and I spent it together. I mean, I had to watch him play football first, of course, but after that it was just me and him. He'd got me flowers, chocolates and a card. I'd got him a card and a funny, dangly football for the rear-view mirror in his car. We hung about and snuggled up in there and kissed, fogging up the windows, with the handbrake jabbing into our sides. I only came home when he told me he had to do his homework.

'You look like you're in love,' Mum whispered as she put my dinner in front of me that evening. I was starting to realise she was right.

The next week, I brought Elliot home to meet my mum and my nan and everybody. I was a bit worried about how he'd react, crammed in there with all of us, but it was cool. I mean, he took up most of Nan's kitchen, but Nan and Mum loved him.

Nan asked him if he wanted a cup of tea.

'Yes please, Mrs Taylor.'

'Isn't he polite?' Nan cooed. 'You can come again.' She loaded a plate with biscuits and was, if I'm honest, a little bit too excited around him. 'He looks like a sports star already, doesn't he?' she said, squeezing Elliot's biceps.

'Nan!'

'Mum, calm down. You're embarrassing him,' my mum added, even though she looked like she agreed.

Elliot just laughed. He seemed so comfortable, like he'd always been sat in Nan's kitchen laughing and chatting with my family.

When he left to go to football practice, Auntie Jean said, 'I didn't know you was into Black guys.'

'Oh my god, what century do you live in, Mum?' Jade said.

'What?' my aunt said dismissively. 'You want to watch out, Emma. Jade's into Black guys too.'

Jade shook her head at her mum. 'What are you on about?'

'Well, you love that Stormzy.'

Jade raised her eyebrows. 'You like Elton John, Mum. Does that mean you're into bald, gay white men?'

Nan cackled. 'I don't want to know the answer to that, Jean. Anyway, Elliot is a lovely fella. Why don't you get a nice bloke like that, Jade?'

'Leave it out, Nan,' Jade said.

The interest in me and Elliot seemed to be building steadily though, and not just in my house. Charlotte and Maisie came up to me after P.E. one day. A rare thing.

'Hi Emma!' Charlotte was super friendly. 'How's it going with Elliot?'

'Great, thanks.' I was on my guard. I'd heard Elliot and Charlotte were old family friends, and it wasn't something I liked much.

'Oh god, he's such a nice guy, isn't he? I've known him since I was three. My dad and his dad were at uni together. It was so sad when he died. Elliot was only eight.'

'I know.' Why was she telling me stuff about my own boyfriend?

'Amy, his mum, and my mum got super close after that.' She pulled her uniform out of her locker breezily and began to get changed. 'So, I guess I'll see you at Amy's fiftieth on Saturday?'

And there it was, out of nowhere. That burning jealousy again, rushing through me. Elliot had told me he was having dinner with his mum and aunt on Saturday for his mum's birthday. He never mentioned she was having a party – or that Charlotte was going to be there.

I decided to confront him about it when we met up after school later that day.

'Why would I mention it, Em? It's just a family dinner,' he said.

'Oh right, so Charlotte is family?' I thought he'd be nice, reassure me, and most importantly, tell me I should come. But he never.

'Like I even know who my mum invited,' he muttered. 'I've got to go. I've got a game. I didn't need this right now, Emma.' And he grabbed his bag and jogged away towards the football pitches.

*

The weekend was torture. Even though he texted a bit, Elliot was hardly in touch. I was really distracted at work at the Bunny Park café. All I could think of was him laughing and eating with Charlotte and his family, and how I wasn't invited.

'Is he ashamed of you or something?' Mum said, which didn't help. I didn't know. It was certainly starting to feel like it.

On Monday at school, Charlotte swished past me in the corridor looking smug. Elliot hadn't called or returned my texts. It burned to know that Charlotte had hung out with him, and that I hadn't even spoken to him.

When I saw him on the football field at lunchtime, my heart was beating so fast. How could it be that we had been so close, so connected, last week, and now I had to fight nerves just to go up to him?

He didn't give me his usual warm grin when he saw me. 'Hey, babe.'

I had a million things to say, but started with the obvious. 'You didn't call me at the weekend.'

He sighed. 'You sent me like a thousand texts. It was my mum's birthday. I was busy.'

I was fighting tears. 'You couldn't just send me one quick text? When you were in the toilet, when you got up in the morning? All of Sunday? It would have taken a second.'

'Listen, Emma, I'm about to start a game. Meet me later? At my car.'

That whole afternoon, I didn't hear a single word a teacher or anyone else said until the bell went and I could go and meet Elliot. My head had helter-skeltered into paranoia, my thoughts all over the place. I'd even started to wonder if his ex, Katie, had been at the party. Had he got back with her?

Finally the school day ended, and we went for a drive.

'You could have texted, just one text!' I wailed. 'You can give me a reason for not calling, can't you?'

Elliot looked angry now. He stopped the car. 'I didn't call you or text you because you messaged me so many times it bugged me, OK?'

I blurted out, 'Was Katie with you?'

'Jesus! What?'

'Oh my god, she was, wasn't she!' I grabbed my phone to find Charlotte's Insta page and to check if she'd posted anything else about his mum's party. Had I missed something when I was stalking it earlier?

'Oh my god, you're being mental.'

Charlotte's Insta had been set to private, which didn't help my paranoia.

'This is mad. You know that?' Elliot was saying. He reached out and held my hand. 'It was just my mum's birthday. We had relatives staying, a load of visitors. I was running around looking after them all, making sure my mum could just enjoy it. I even baked a cake! I wanted to do everything I could to make sure she had the best fiftieth. I didn't think. OK?'

I felt a bit stupid about making a drama out of his mum's big day. 'OK, I'm sorry,' I said and let go of his hand to reach over and hug him. I lowered my voice a bit, hoping I sounded seductive. 'Can we go back to yours?'

He shook his head. 'My mum took the day off today. She'll be home.'

I exhaled. 'When are you going to tell her about me?'

He took my hand again and squeezed it. 'My mum's cool, Emma. She's the best. But she's just a bit weird about . . . people from the estate. That sounds bad, I know, but I swear, she's not a snob. I just need to find a good time.'

'That *is* being a snob, though,' I said. My mum was right. Elliot was ashamed of me.

'No! Mum's not like that, I promise you. She raised me by herself after my dad passed away, and—'

'So did mine,' I snapped.

He sighed. 'I know, but—'

'But what?'

He was clearly trying to find the right words that would cause me the least harm. 'She has this vision that I'll end up marrying a girl who's a doctor or a lawyer.'

'And not a scrubber like me?' Just by being who I was, coming from where I was from, his mum thought I'd get him into trouble? I felt like I'd swallowed a stone.

Elliot gave me another hug. 'Ah, don't be like that. I told you, I just need to pick my moment. You got to understand. She just wants the best for me.'

'And that's not me?' I said stiffly.

'I never said that.'

He didn't need to. I didn't talk right; I didn't look right. I slept on the floor at my nan's house on an estate. My dad wasn't an accountant; he hadn't died of natural causes like Elliot's had. My dad, my family, weren't respectable. I couldn't help any of it. The whole thing really hurt.

'The mad thing is,' I told Soreya and Matilda later, 'my mum's the same. She wouldn't let me hang out with the kids from my old estate in case I ended up like *them*.'

'That's not right,' Matilda said. 'An estate – any estate – is just a place where people live. Ordinary people.'

Soreya agreed. 'Yeah. It's not like "estate people" are a particular breed.'

'Although,' Matilda added, flicking my thick long ponytail, 'Emma's definitely part squirrel.'

That did make me smile a bit as I smacked her hand away.

'Don't worry about Elliot's mum,' Matilda went on. 'Who cares what she thinks of you?'

I cared. His mum's opinion of me mattered because it obviously mattered to *Elliot*. He loved his mum. All his dreams included buying a house for her and making her proud.

For a week I didn't say anything else about it. It was hard, really hard, but I needed to be cool and not push him. And finally, there was a glimmer of light. He invited me over to have supper with him and his mum.

'Oh for god's sake, Emma, just be yourself,' Nan said, watching as I tried on different clothes with shaking hands and sweaty palms. 'You're not having tea with the bloody Queen.'

No, I wasn't. This was a much bigger deal.

In the end I wore dark jeans and a black polo neck I borrowed off my mum that she got for job interviews. I wanted something that totally covered my boobs.

Amy Gonzales was serious-looking and small. Elliot towered over her. He gave me encouraging looks, but I could tell he was nervous, too. I couldn't speak. I don't mean I was quiet. I mean, I literally couldn't speak.

We sat awkwardly in the living room and drank the tea Amy had served in cups with saucers. Tea cooled so quickly in a small cup, so I drained mine and sat my empty cup and saucer down on the table before Elliot and his mum had even touched theirs.

'Would you like some more? You can help yourself. The pot is in the kitchen,' Amy said. 'I dare say you already know your way around my home,' she added, pressing her lips together a bit.

I had to have turned bright red, and tried to say, 'I'm all right thanks,' but it just came out in a weird croak. What was the matter with me? Why was I just sitting there like an idiot, too scared to talk?

I sighed with relief when Amy went into the kitchen to finish making dinner.

'You OK?' Elliot asked, reaching over to hold my hand.

I nodded silently. His chatty girlfriend had turned into an idiot zombie.

We had dinner, and it was OK. Amy mainly talked to Elliot, asked him about school, laughed at his jokes. She pretty much ignored me, so I just sat there on mute. The only thing I said was, 'Thank you for having me.' Even that, I mumbled.

'Be a gentleman and drive the lady home, son,' she told Elliot.

I felt a rush of relief as we stepped out of his house, and he held my hand as we walked over to the car.

'I never thought I'd see you so quiet! Was my mum that scary?' Elliot laughed, but I could tell he really was puzzled.

'Oh my god,' I said, hot with embarrassment. 'I'm so sorry. I just shut down. I thought anything I said would sound stupid. Does your mum think I'm an idiot?'

Elliot pulled me to him and kissed my head. 'You worry too much.'

When we got to my house, I asked him to come in.

'Taste of my own medicine, eh?' he joked.

I shook my head. Mum was out on a date and probably wouldn't be home till really late. Nan would be in bed and the others wouldn't come in the front room where we slept. It was risky, but I needed this to work out. So he came in, and I looked down at him for a moment as I led the way up the stairs. Elliot was beautiful. His face, his eyes, his lips . . . I just wanted this to work out. I wanted to make him happy.

We sat on the sofa and kissed. I let his hand wander up inside my poloneck. We'd done quite a lot of stuff, but never gone all the way.

'I really want to now . . .' I whispered to him.

'Here?' he said.

'No one will come in, I promise.'

He kissed me hard, and lay on top of me on the sofa, but as he was kissing me more and putting his hands in my jeans, trying to get them off, I suddenly felt this fear. Like a real terror. Things hadn't been good the last couple of weeks. I'd felt so insecure – and now doing this, like this, on my nan's sofa? It wasn't right.

'Hang on. Stop a sec.' I pulled myself up and he sat back.

'What's wrong?' He was almost panting.

'Nothing,' I told him, suddenly feeling stupid. 'I . . . I just need to stop. I'm sorry. I feel weird. I'm sorry,' I repeated.

'Did I do something wrong? Did I hurt you?'

I shook my head. 'No no, you didn't, I just . . . This just doesn't feel right. I'm not ready. I thought I was, but I'm not.'

'OK.' He breathed out heavily. 'I'd better go then.' He got up, straightening himself out.

I jumped up, a bit panicky now. 'Please, you don't have to go! We can just snuggle up for bit on the sofa and—'

'Emma, I've got to go. My head's all over the place.' He scratched his face and looked at me. 'I'll be honest. This whole thing has got weird. The way you were acting at my mum's, and what happened just now . . . Maybe we both need a bit of space?'

I was *definitely* panicking now. He was changing his mind about me. 'No, no, I don't need space,' I told him quickly, reaching up to kiss him.

'Emma, honestly,' he began, but I kissed him again until he kissed me back, and we sank back on to the sofa.

'I'm sorry,' I whispered. 'Please stay.'

He did stay, and we had sex on my nan's sofa. I tried to shake away the feelings I'd had before, that it wasn't quite right. I just shut my eyes.

When we finished, Elliot kissed me and lay smiling with his head on my lap for a while. I stroked his head, his cheek. I wanted to be lost in it all, but I was nervous about people coming home and finding us. I wished we'd waited for somewhere more private, but I didn't want him to think I didn't want to do it. It was too risky. He'd just talk about taking a break again.

I could suddenly hear Soreya in my head saying, 'But you *didn't* want to.'

'Was it "consent" or "enthusiastic consent"?' Matilda's voice this time.

I pushed both voices away.

'That didn't hurt, did it?' Elliot asked when he eventually sat up to go.

'No. Why would it?'

He kissed my face so gently before he answered. 'Apparently it does with some girls the first time.'

It didn't occur to me to lie. 'It wasn't my first time.'

I felt his body freeze and he was still and quiet for a minute. Then he pulled away from our cuddle and looked down at me. Not angry, exactly, but serious. 'What?'

'It wasn't my first time,' I said again, more cautiously now.

'Why didn't you tell me?'

'You never asked,' I said.

I paused. 'Does it matter?'

His jaw tensed. 'Who else have you been with? How many?'

'How many have *you* been with?' I asked, sitting up with a bit of a frown. I reached for my clothes and started to put them back on.

'You're my second,' he said.

'Right. And you're *my* second. Are we done now?'

We got dressed. Both of us were quiet. I didn't know what I had done to make him . . . not angry, more disappointed. Like he was disgusted.

'Emma,' he finally said. 'I gotta ask who.'

I exhaled hard. 'It was Mo, from my year.'

He narrowed his eyes. 'Mo Mahmood? I used to play football with him. Why would you bang such a creep?'

I started feeling annoyed. 'Elliot, I'm sorry, but that's not your business. I never told you I was a virgin. You assumed. Anyhow, I only dated him for about a week or something, and it only happened once.'

'Just a week, and you fucked him?'

My jaw hung open for a moment. 'Oh my god! It wasn't like that. It was a different thing. A mistake.'

'Oh. You *accidently* fucked him? You've been with me for more than a month, but you were like "I wanna wait".' He mocked my voice and flapped his hand in the air. 'But you let that creep shag you immediately? Sorry Emma, but I can't look at you right now.'

And he didn't. He looked around the room, finding his jacket and his keys. I couldn't understand that one minute he was holding me tight and covering my face with gentle little kisses, and the next he was grabbing his things and heading for the door. I tried to speak but I started to cry. I stood in front of the door so he couldn't open it.

'It happened too fast with Mo; it wasn't right. I didn't want to make the same mistake again. Please!' I croaked.

'Move away from the door, Emma.'

'OK, but please, please listen—'

'All I'm hearing is that you slept with a scumbag like him straight away and you basically lied to me about things being special with us. Out of my way.' He pulled me away from the door.

I was crying so hard. 'Can you please just listen?' I begged, running down the stairs in a state, following him. 'I didn't know you then! I wish I had. I wish it had never happened with Mo. I love you, Elliot! I love you so much! Elliot, please! Please!'

He ignored me, got into his car and left. I stood there uselessly in the car park, and cried and cried, not even caring who saw.

After a while, I went back upstairs. Nan appeared, smoking and making tea.

'Well, that was a racket. You all right?'

I shook my head, went into the front room and lay on my mattress on the floor, sobbing and sobbing until I fell asleep.

EIGHTEEN

He dumped me the next morning, on Whatsapp, when I was on my way to school. No phone call, no talking about it, just a message.

Emma, we're done. I can't see you again. Don't call me.

I couldn't believe this was happening to me again, after what had happened with Mo.

I did call him – of course I did. I called him ten times, each message more frantic and teary than the one before. All his lessons were in the sixth-form block so it was easy for him to avoid me. Year Elevens like me weren't allowed in there.

I went to his house after school. I couldn't function until I'd spoken to him, and I couldn't stop crying. I rang the doorbell and knocked, but no one answered the door. I called out, 'Elliot! Elliot!' until his mum came out.

'Have a bit of dignity, my dear,' she said. 'This is part of growing up. If Elliot doesn't want you, he doesn't want you. I have neighbours, please stop shouting.'

'Please Amy!' I wept. 'Please, will you talk to him for me? I love him so much. Will you tell him?'

She looked at me with pity, and for a second I thought she would invite me in, but she just said, 'I'm sorry. He doesn't want to see you. You must respect that.' She paused, looking me up and down. 'Stick with your own kind, OK?' And she closed the door in my face.

Stick with your own kind? *Trash.* She'd basically called me trash.

Somehow I made it home. Mum took one look at me, grabbed my phone and texted Soreya and Matilda.

Girls, this is Emma's mum. We need an army. Boy troubles.

'You need your mates around when your heart's been broken,' she told me.

I'd already cried on Soreya and Matilda at school all day long, but they came round anyway to perch on the sofa. If Soreya was in any way relieved that Elliot had dumped me, she didn't show it, which I really appreciated. They were especially shocked when I told them what Elliot's mum had said.

'That is completely out of order,' declared Matilda. 'Like, isn't that racist?'

Soreya raised an eyebrow. 'Uh, no, I don't think so. Anyway, she meant your own people as in "rough".'

'Nice, Soreya,' Matilda said. 'You're rough, Emma, in case you didn't know.'

Soreya hit her with a cushion.

'It's true though,' I said with a deep sigh. 'I'm not the sort of girl he wants to end up with.' I could feel myself about to cry again.

Soreya grabbed the toilet roll on the table, handing it to me. 'No,' she corrected. '*He's* not the sort of guy *you* want to end up with. I get judged all the time because I'm Muslim. It's not all that different, his mum judging you 'cos of your class. The important thing is that you don't *believe* the judgements they make. Trust who you are – that's what my mum says. But, like, in Somali.'

Mum brought us squash and biscuits. 'Here you go, girls. Emma, your nan is going to be in here in twenty minutes to watch *EastEnders* . . .'

'I *so* want my own room again,' I told Matilda and Soreya when Mum had gone. 'My mum's saving up for a deposit so we can move, and I'm doing what I can with the money I'm making from the café on Saturdays. I'll have a big house one day, mate, I'm telling you. You'll have to take your shoes off when you come in because the carpets will be so lush.'

'I already do that,' Soreya said, pointing to her shoes by the door.

Matilda smiled at me. 'What're you going to do, Emma? Be a movie star?'

I shrugged. 'Maybe.'

'I can see the careers advisor being really helpful with that,' Soreya said. 'She'll get you work experience with a plumbing firm.'

I pursed my lips. 'To be honest, I'll do anything if it means we can move,' I said. 'I love my mum, but Jesus – sharing a room with her? I can't even bring a guy back and have a bit of privacy.'

I trailed off. The one time I'd done that, it hadn't worked out so well, had it?

*

Over the next few days, what felt like a million times a day, I thought about Elliot. My chest hurt. My heart ached. I wanted to speak to him, even if I couldn't get him back. I just wanted him to acknowledge me. Every time I thought I saw him about, my heart would stop – but a lot of the time it wouldn't be him, just someone else who was tall, or Black, or just a bloke in the corner of my eye. The few times when I actually *did* see him, he fully blanked me, and he ghosted every message I sent. I don't even know if he got them. I think he blocked my number.

I couldn't sleep. I lay awake all night, listening to my mum snoring and thinking of ways to get to Elliot. Maybe

Charlotte would talk to him for me? Charlotte, like all of the Charlottes, was too posh and polite to be horrible to my face.

The next day at lunch, I just came out with it. 'I need to talk to you about Elliot,' I said.

Charlotte tossed her long, blonde hair, glancing at her friends at the nearby table. 'What do you mean?'

'Has he said anything to you about me?'

'Don't you think you should be talking to *him* if you two have an issue?'

I shook my head, exasperated. 'Look, he won't talk to me—'

'I honestly don't know, Emma,' she interrupted. 'He doesn't really talk about this sort of thing. He's a private guy. Look, this is shit for you, I get it. It's shit that he won't talk to you.'

Tears started prickling my eyelids again. 'It was fine until he found out about Mo. Then he dumped me.'

Charlotte put her arm around me. 'Boys are weird. They've got delicate little egos, and he obviously couldn't stand someone else being around before him. That's not cool. And that's on him. You've done nothing wrong.'

What she said was actually helping. And then there I was, in the corner of the canteen with Charlotte, crying and blowing my nose. She put her tray down and hugged me properly. She smelled of a freshly run bath, clean and like fruity soap suds. I shed a few more tears, before straightening up and wiping them away. People around pretended not to look.

I needed to get a grip.

*

Later, at home, I grabbed my phone while I could use the neighbours' wifi and decided to go live on Insta to talk about how I felt. The flat was quiet for once, and it sort of felt like recording a video diary.

'What are you meant to do with all the love you have for someone when they don't want it any more?' I said, watching my tear-streaked face on my screen. 'I feel like all this love I had for him is sitting inside me, turning to sadness.' I didn't say Elliot's name, but I knew most people would figure out who I meant. 'I know he doesn't want me any more, but it was all just so quick, so sudden that my heart still thinks it's his, and it's like it keeps banging itself into this brick wall. Even though my *mind* understands he doesn't want me any more, my heart doesn't get it. It keeps battering itself again and again, till I think I might actually die from the pain.'

I took a deep breath, then ended the live feed. I kept the recording – #heartache #heartbreak – and posted it.

NINETEEN

It had felt good to get things off my chest that night. But it didn't mean that things were any easier at school, especially in the countdown to our exams.

Mr Johnson, the French teacher, was rubbish at controlling the class. Ellie knew this. So, that day, she decided that she was looking for a fight – again.

First I knew about it was when something hit my cheek. A little ball of tissue, rolled tight with spit and blown through a McDonalds straw. I looked around and saw Ellie laughing with one of her gang.

'Just leave it,' Matilda whispered to me.

But I'd left it last time, and it had got me nowhere. I enough of her, of the school, of *everything*. I stood up and went over to her desk.

'Have you got something to say, Ellie?'

She was surprised. Mr Johnson might not be good at

controlling the class, but he was still a teacher and could see what was going on. She hadn't thought I'd confront her in front of a teacher.

'I don't talk to slags,' she muttered.

I bent down so we were face-to-face and gobbed, hard, right in her stupid face.

There was a scream from Ellie, a *whooaaa* of delight in the drama from some of the kids, and some flapping from Mr Johnson. But nothing from me. I picked up my bag, left the class and just went home.

Freedom. No regrets.

Matilda had been right. Spitting counted as assault. That's what Mrs Sharma said on the phone when my mum was called in to the head's office.

'Should have reported her when she did it to me then, shouldn't I?' I said when my mum hung up the call, staring at me with her hands on her hips. 'I wish I'd punched her.' I didn't care about being like Dad any more. I didn't care about anything.

Mum brought me in to school the next morning, muttering about having had to make an excuse about a doctor's appointment to her boss to get the time off. Mrs Sharma was stony-faced.

'This is a very serious matter. I don't think you quite appreciate the trouble you're in, Emma.'

I sat back on my chair as Mrs Sharma talked to Mum

about what could be done with me. My mum looked so self-conscious and out of her comfort zone that Mrs Sharma could have been saying, 'We're going to have to take Emma to London Zoo and feed her to the crocodiles,' and she would still have sat there, nodding blankly in agreement.

Despite being there to get a massive bollocking, I loved being in Mrs Sharma's office. It was warm, and had nice pictures on the wall, along with a load of certificates. One wall was just books, from top to bottom. It smelled of coffee, and of the life of a person who had their shit together.

I wondered if Mrs Sharma had children. I couldn't see any photos on her desk. I bet if she did, her kids wouldn't have spat in anyone's face. Someone with an office like this didn't have children who spat. She had an accent, Mrs Sharma. Indian. Only slightly. She wasn't born here, but she was head of the school. I wondered if Auntie Jean would have something to say about that.

'Emma, I know you've had a difficult time. I understand you have been targeted by bullies,' Mrs Sharma was saying. 'We take bullying very seriously at this school.'

'How come Ellie hasn't been expelled then?' I asked.

My mum turned red. She may have thought we were better than everyone back on Nan's estate, but here, in Mrs Sharma's office, it was a whole other world where she barely had the confidence to open her mouth. But I decided I did. If you didn't speak up, then you would never have a nice office that smelled of coffee or a wall full of books, or a pretty tin dustbin with birds on it under your desk. You'd always find yourself sleeping on other people's sofas and floors. I didn't want to use one dusty teabag to make two cups of tea for the rest of my life. I wanted my own teabag every time.

Plus, it was painful watching my mum in that room. At one point I thought she was going to get up, find a cloth and start cleaning.

'I'm well aware of Ellie and how she has made you a target,' said Mrs Sharma. 'We talk to one another here. We have spoken to other pupils in complete confidence, who have told us what has been going on.'

That was news. What other pupils? Maybe Matilda and Soreya? I never thought any kid would dare snitch on Ellie, but apparently . . .

'Mrs Hamilton, do you talk with Emma about what goes on for her at school?' Mrs Sharma asked.

Mum straightened up, swallowing a bit. 'Emma had a boyfriend who dumped her. She's been very upset.'

For god's sake! As if I wanted Mrs Sharma to know that. My cheeks were pink now.

'It's all right. I'm over it,' I muttered.

'You're not.' Mum turned to Mrs Sharma. 'She still cries herself to sleep sometimes.'

God, I needed my own room.

Mrs Sharma drew in a long breath. 'All that said, spitting at another pupil is unacceptable, no matter how they have behaved. If there is something upsetting you, you tell a teacher. Is that understood?'

'Yes, miss.'

And that was it.

I was suspended for a week. I had expected a bigger punishment, but Mrs Sharma kept talking about my exams and 'the future'. I didn't want to stay in the flat all week, but I had no money to do anything, and everyone else was at school.

Nan was like, 'Bloody hell, we don't need this on top of everything!' Becca and Jade had both just been arrested for shoplifting and were facing charges.

'I'm not going back to that school,' I told Mum.

'Oh yeah?' She folded her arms. 'And what if they tell the social?'

I looked down at the worn carpet when she said that. We were all frightened of the social and the council, whether it was them finding out about the cash in hand work, or how many people lived at the flat.

'You know, there was a time I was terrified they'd take you into care. When I thought I might go to prison, after your dad . . .' Mum trailed off.

'Don't be daft,' Nan said. 'We'd have had her.'

Mum suddenly looked furious. 'That's not what you said at the time!'

Jean chipped in. 'Oh, here she goes again. No one does enough for her; no one cares about her. You have no idea how hard it was for Mum when you was all over the news!'

Mum brought it up later, still fuming.

'It's not natural, Emma,' she said to me as we settled down to bed. 'Living with your sister when you're an adult. Not sure how natural it is at any point, to be honest.'

I ended up basically having a whole week to myself while I was suspended. I helped Mum with some cleaning jobs, but I spent most of my time taking pictures of myself and putting them up on my Insta page. It was hard to make Nan's flat look nice – I had to pick my background carefully. Becca let me take photos on her bed sometimes, or I did it when she wasn't about. That was much better.

'You know I want commission if anyone wants to sell anything on your site, don't you?' she joked whenever she spotted one of those pics.

I had over five hundred followers now. A lot of pervs, to be fair, but more and more girls messaging me positive things – saying they loved my hair, my figure and that video I'd kept up from my Live, talking about heartbreak.

I was just rewatching that video on my feed when out of the blue, Elliot messaged me. My heart jumped sky-high. Adrenaline roared through me. I almost dropped my phone trying to open the message.

Get checked out. You've given me chlamydia.

That was all it said. He was blaming me, of course. That was literally all that the guy I'd been spending my time crying over had to say to me.

Nan covered Mum's cleaning job so she could come with me to the clinic. 'I can't face going on my own, Mum, please?'

And so she'd agreed, and we got on the bus to the hospital. I kept looking at Elliot's text, reading it again and again in case I missed something, a clue that he might still have feelings for me. In the end Mum grabbed my phone and put it in her bag saying, 'Enough is enough, Emma.'

We walked through the maze of clinical corridors to find the right department. 'Oh, this is just not the sort of place I ever wanted you to end up,' she said when we got to the wing of the hospital where people who hadn't used a condom sat staring at their feet.

'I haven't "ended up" here, Mum,' I said, folding my arms as we sat in the plastic chairs. 'It's a clinic, not a brothel.'

Mum picked up an old magazine and started to read it. It was so old that the celebrity couple getting married on the front cover were divorced now. I waited, clutching my appointment number.

Finally, it was my turn.

The nurse asked a lot of questions. 'When did you have sex? What contraception did you use?' And then a few intense ones – ones that meant I was glad I'd left Mum in the waiting area. 'Is there anyone in your life you're afraid of?' No, I thought. Not any more.

She took a swab and blood test, and told me I had to start taking the antibiotics even though the test result wouldn't be back for a few days, just to make sure.

I had to go to the waiting area again and wait for the prescription, then to the pharmacy to get the pills.

'Emma Hamilton?' the woman at the pharmacy counter asked.

Mum looked up first. 'Yes, that's my daughter.'

I looked up then at the woman behind the counter.

Amy Gonzales didn't blink as she handed me the antibiotics, along with a little paper bag full of condoms.

I wished I could just disappear and die. My face was absolutely on fire. I could barely look up as I left.

You'd think a day like that wouldn't have the imagination to get any worse. But as I walked away from Elliot's mum at the pharmacy counter, I was so flustered I literally slammed into Ellie.

She looked as horrified to be caught outside the clinic as I was. We didn't say a word. We both just shuffled on.

*

Back at school a week later, Ellie came to find me. I came out of the loo and she was there.

'Are you gonna tell anyone?' she said.

'Eh?' At first I had no idea what she was on about.

Her face was white. 'Have you told anyone about seeing me at the clinic?'

I started washing my hands. 'No,' I said shortly.

Ellie had a look I'd never seen on her face before. She looked *scared*. I had never seen her with a boy, or ever heard any gossip about her and a boy. She never looked like she would even *like* a boy, to be honest.

'I don't even know if I've got anything,' I added, curious now. 'They make you take the pills before you get the result.'

'I know,' Ellie said.

'Have you got something?' I asked.

Ellie nodded.

'Chlamydia?'

She nodded again and picked up her bag. 'We're all right now,' she muttered. 'OK?'

And that was it, apparently. We were OK.

TWENTY

Bumping into Ellie at that clinic turned out to be a good thing, as it meant she wasn't trying to kill me any more. But the minute things got a bit better at school, things at home got really messy.

Becca and Jade's dad, the perv, came to stay again. The arguments with Auntie Jean were off the scale. I was massively relieved when Mum suggested we go and stay at Suze's new flat while he was there.

Suze had moved off the Elsworth estate and was renting the flat above her café. I immediately wished I could live in the flat for good.

'Oh my god, Suze, I love it!' I said once we'd dropped off all our stuff. It had two little bedrooms, a bathroom and kitchen, and then this massive living room. There was an iron staircase outside that led up to it from a tiny courtyard garden.

Downstairs, Suze had decked out the tiny café in retro furniture. She'd got a loan from the bank, and the place was doing OK. She looked really happy, buzzing.

When Mum went to bed that night, I stayed up a bit. Suze poured me a glass of wine with a wink, and asked me, 'So how are things for you *really*, Emma?'

I told her everything. From Ellie, to Mo, to Elliot, to the clap clinic . . . To the fact that I was still having nightmares where Dad was screaming at me and chasing me and I was begging him to forgive me.

Suze reckoned I had post-traumatic stress disorder.

'Isn't that what soldiers get after wars?' I asked.

'Well, haven't you been in a bit of a war?'

All that week after school, I helped Suze in her café. I was used to coffee machines and serving customers at the Bunny Park café on Saturdays. I had the best week I'd had in a long time. No drama, no sleeping on a sofa. Just helping Suze. But once Nan texted to say Bertie the Pervert had gone, Mum started packing our bag to go back.

'Can't we stay, Mum?' I begged. 'With Suze?'

'No. I agreed with Suze it was just one week, and we can't take the piss.'

So we went back to Nan's and the cramped living room.

*

Getting suspended wasn't something you could come back from. It tainted you. You were rough. You were bad news. You had seriously messed up. It was like everything Elliot's mum had thought about me coming true.

Matilda and Soreya stuck by me, of course, but as far as a lot of other people – including teachers – were concerned, I'd proved them all right. I was one of those people who ended up with drama and trouble whatever they did.

Charlotte might have hugged me that time, but when I tried to talk to her, she just gave me a cool smile: tight, quick, and mostly towards her feet. Even in Drama club.

Drama was the only thing keeping me going. I wrote a show that I hoped could be used partly for my exam score, and made sure there was a part for every kid in Drama club. I stayed behind with Mrs Delerosh and planned how we were going to stage it.

'Emma, in my eyes you are already a superstar! Never have I had a pupil who thinks so big!'

Mrs Delerosh talked to me like we only existed in that moment. Drama with her felt like the only place, apart from Suze's café, where I knew exactly what I was doing, and was completely and utterly comfortable.

*

'You and Emma need to get a place of your own,' Auntie Jean said one night, out of the blue. 'She won't say it to your face, but it's hard for Mum. You two aren't bringing much in, always squirrelling money away, not contributing. This isn't a hotel. Sorry, but someone had to say it.'

I wasn't having that. 'How much do you and your girls bring in then, Auntie Jean?' It was the first time I'd ever really answered her back.

'Keep out of this, Emma,' Jean snarled at me.

Mum had been trying to keep the peace lately, but she lost it now. 'Don't you dare talk to Emma like that,' she shouted. '*She* brings money in. She's sixteen and has a job, while your kids go around nicking things and getting into trouble with the police. You've been sponging off Mum for *years!*'

Jean's face went all blotchy. 'SPONGING? That's all you've done since you got here. Who asked you to come here anyhow? Why did you have to run away? You can't even keep a man without killing him!'

Mum gave a nasty laugh. 'You think that lazy pervy scumbag coming round here 'cos he's run out of money is "keeping a man"? You're having a laugh.'

They ended up lashing out with actual slaps, and didn't stop till Nan waded in and separated them. I watched like it was all happening on the telly, or in slow motion or something. I thought of Mrs Delerosh and Mrs Sharma and Miss Macey and all my teachers at school. Did they have families like this? Did Ellie? Did Soreya? Did Charlotte? Was this normal?

When everything calmed down, Nan told Mum she'd never kick us out. 'But you got to admit,' she said, 'it'd be easier for you to get another place to live than Jean. You've only got one kid. Jean has two . . .'

Jean's kids were both legally adults. But Mum didn't say this, neither did I.

*

I knew I had to step it up. So as well as my weekend café job, on Tuesday and Wednesday afternoons I got extra cleaning jobs of my own for which I had to lie about my age.

Matilda found this sort of funny. 'Most people lie about their age to get into a club or a bar to buy booze, but you do it to clean people's loos.'

I tried not to feel offended.

'Fair play though,' Soreya weighed in, and I felt a bit better. 'You're helping your mum out. But exams are coming really soon now, Emma. You gotta have time to revise.'

I didn't care about that. I was getting eight pounds an hour, cash. At two lots of three hours, that was almost fifty quid a week – a bit for the phone bill and the electricity, and a decent bit of food. And most importantly, I had extra to put towards a deposit for our own place.

'If I could leave school and work full time, we'd be sorted, Mum,' I said to her one evening.

The teachers for all my subjects were on at me because I was lagging and my work wasn't finished. I'd run out of excuses, and time. The only coursework I did was for Mrs Delerosh, who said the monologue I wrote for Drama was a 'masterpiece'.

'Thanks, miss. Do you think I can submit it as my Maths coursework too?' I joked.

When everyone else had left the room, Mrs Delerosh held me back.

'I heard from your tutor you are behind in all your other classes,' she said, sitting at her desk. 'What is going on, Emma? Why is your school work collapsing? You're a clever girl.'

I had no answer for her.

I started missing days from school to do cleaning work instead. I didn't even tell Mum. The less time I spent at school, the more money I made. My clients had friends, and now I cleaned for them as well. They all had big, fancy houses. I'd swan around sometimes in between the scrubbing and pretend they were mine.

On the days when I wasn't cleaning, and did go to school, I was tired. All I kept thinking about was the money I could be making if I wasn't there.

Soreya knew what I was up to. 'You're gonna fail your GCSEs, you know, if you keep missing school,' she scolded.

This was the only thing Soreya was judgemental about. The stuff with my mum, Mo, Elliot, and even getting chlamydia, I could tell her and she was supportive. But my missing school was the line for her. 'My mum and dad came here for a better life, to give me a good education. I'm not wasting my opportunities. If you do, Emma, then you're mad.'

'But if I'm working and making money, what's wrong with that?' I argued. 'Obviously I don't want to be a cleaner all my life, but it's a means to an end.'

'Oi!' Soreya said. 'My favourite auntie's a cleaner.'

'Yeah, well, so is my mum, but it's not what you wanna be, is it?'

'True,' she said. 'But they're are working hard so girls like us have something better to aim for, yeah? Like, if you're going to leave school, then what's your mum been busting a gut for all these years?'

'You've seen where I live,' I said sulkily. 'We're like refugees.'

Soreya pulled a face. 'Do you know how refugees actually live?'

'Oh god, I was only joking.'

'Yeah well, it's not funny. Honestly, Emma, some of their stories would make you cry.' She sighed. 'You don't get how lucky you are, compared to a lot of people.'

Soreya had her own bedroom. Her parents both worked

full time but her dad was always home straight after work. You went to her house and her mum was always smiling, making you food. She was really good in school. She even got pocket money sometimes.

'Soreya, I haven't got a dad!' I said. 'I sleep on my nan's sofa. You don't have to deal with what I have to deal with.'

She rolled her eyes. 'People shout at my mum to "go home" on the streets, even when she's with my little brother and sisters. People blame Somalians for crimes before anything is proven. They don't do that to you. And yeah, I get that I don't have to deal with some of the stuff *you* have to deal with, but this ain't a competition about who's worse off. All I know is, the better education you get, the more options you have, better opportunities. And you're taking yours for granted.'

I shook my head, ticked off now. 'You're getting too deep, Soreya.'

Next, it was Matilda's turn to have her say about my life. 'It's not like you're not clever. You are,' she told me. 'You could definitely get into college. It's only a couple of years.'

A couple of years was too long. I'd told them that before. I needed a life, now. A life where no one had to go to a food bank for extra grub, and no one's nan leaned over the sofa to hoover it while they were still asleep on it.

There was no point in any of it.

I just walked out some days. I'd go into school to register, then bunk off. If I didn't do that, then it was easy for me to email some excuse from my mum's account. As long as they had a message from her, I got away with it. Maybe they had just given up chasing up on me now the end of school was near. I ignored the disappointed looks on my teachers' faces on the rare occasions I did turn up.

In between cleaning jobs, I hung out in the park. The weather was warm now, and some older girls I knew a bit hung out there, too. They offered me weed, and though I didn't like smoking it, it was an excuse to hang out with them and chat. Sitting around in parks smoking weed was what losers did, I knew that. But I had no other friends that were around, and I didn't want to hang out at Nan's.

One night, when I got back, my head swimming a little, Nan and Jean were waiting.

'You've been bunking off, haven't you?' Nan started the minute I walked in. 'Becca's seen you down the park with the Mortimer estate lot when you should have been at school.'

I shrugged.

Nan said, 'Emma, I can't have you here if all you're gonna do is doss. I can't, darling. It's hard enough as it is.'

But she shut up about me skipping school when she found

out I had so many jobs. Then she asked Mum for more housekeeping.

I was furious. I was making that money for me and Mum, not my nan. I was getting closer to being able to get us out of there once and for all. I could feel it.

We needed to go.

TWENTY-ONE

A couple of days later, two men came up to me as I was leaving the park to go to one of my cleaning jobs. They were smartly dressed. I was on my own, and looked at them warily.

'Excuse me,' one of them said. He had a really nice smile. 'We work for a modelling agency, and you've really got a look a lot of our clients would be after. You're stunning, seriously. I hope that's OK to say?'

He put his hands up to show he didn't mean to offend me or anything. I looked him up and down. He didn't look like a weirdo or a pervert. He was actually really good-looking.

'What's your name?' he asked.

'Emma,' I told him.

He gave me a card, a proper business card. It had his name, logo and an address and everything. These guys were legit.

'That's me, Joe, at Topaz Models,' he said. 'I was a model myself, you know.'

'Till he got too old.' The other man winked. He looked younger than Joe, really tall with long dark hair that he kept sweeping back.

'Thanks, mate,' Joe said. 'But yeah. Now I run my own agency with Zane here. He saw you and thought you're just what we are looking for. Have you modelled before?'

I laughed. 'No, I haven't.'

'Why's that funny?' Joe said. 'It's surprising, to be honest. We saw you and thought someone was bound to have snapped you up already.'

I shook my head shyly.

'Looks like we're in with a chance, then, Joe,' Zane said with a little wink. 'Emma, we think you have massive potential as a model. You interested?'

Interested? I nearly screamed! Thank god I kept it in. This man, this professional scout, thought that I had what it took to be a *model*. It was like the answer to my prayers. I nodded like an idiot.

Zane pumped his fists. 'Yeah! I'm so happy you haven't already got an agent.'

I felt dizzy. *Was this actually happening?* Oh god, I couldn't speak!

'We'd really like you to come to our studio and have some

professional pictures taken,' Joe was saying. 'And we'll go from there, yeah?'

'What . . . what should I wear?' I blurted out. God, I knew I'd sound stupid.

Joe took out his wallet and opened it. My eyes were on stalks. It was stuffed full of cash, like in a film or something. I had never seen so much money in my life. He took out two fifty-pound notes and handed them to me.

'Here. An early investment,' he said with a smile. 'Buy yourself something nice. Something that shows off your figure. Come along tomorrow.'

Then they jumped in their car and went off.

I stood there like a melon. Two men had just come along and handed me a hundred quid. I'd have to clean for about fifteen hours to get that. I couldn't breathe, I was that excited. What time did they want me tomorrow? I looked at the card. There was a phone number. I'd text and ask. *No.* That was lame, uncool. I couldn't text right away, either, it was too soon. But it wasn't a date. It was work. So maybe it was OK. I'd wait till I got home. I couldn't wait to tell Mum.

When I did, she was as excited but cautious. 'They looked all right?' she asked, her brows knitting a bit. 'You sure they weren't just weirdos?'

I showed her the business card. 'They were smartly dressed and one of them was really good-looking,' I reassured her.

'Was he now?' she said, taking the card. 'Well,' she said. 'That looks proper.'

I texted Joe to ask what time. Really quickly a text came back.

4pm x

I was going places. Finally, it was starting to come together.

*

Mum came with me to the shops the very next morning, even though it was a Thursday and she knew I was meant to be in school. She had the morning off. It was so amazing to know I could buy anything I wanted. I got this black sequin dress with spaghetti straps. It was ultra short and it came down really low at the front.

'My bra is crap though, Mum.' I could see the top of it peeking over the dress. So we bought a new bra for me, and I had enough left over for knickers to go with it, too.

'You sure this is OK?' I said, twirling in front of Mum in my new outfit.

She clasped her hands together. 'Oh darling, you really look the part. Dead classy.'

I had a shoe problem though. None of mine looked right with the dress. Luckily, Mum had a pair of black stilettos. They were a bit scuffed, but we got a marker pen and coloured them in. You couldn't tell, as long as you didn't look too closely.

I'd barely slept the previous night, I was so nervous and excited. After the shopping trip, I had a shower and spent ages scrunching my hair while it dried to get the big curls. I clipped a few strands up at the side and let the rest tumble around my face. Then I put on my make-up: loads of thick eyelashes, but I did the rest of my face quite subtly, no mad blusher or contouring – but I did put on red lipstick.

'Oh my god, my baby looks beautiful!' Mum gasped. Then she insisted on coming with me. 'I won't actually come in and cramp your style. I'll sit at the bus stop till you come out,' she said.

'All right,' I said, glad she was coming.

I sort of expected the building to be a bit more flash. Like a proper photography studio or office or something. But it was just a house. A terrace, with a broken step leading to the front door. The gate was off its hinges and lying flat in the front garden, which was covered in weeds. The door was blue, the paint peeling.

I glanced back towards the bus stop, which was only a little way down the road. 'Don't let them see you, Mum,' I called to her. 'I want to look like a superstar, not your baby.'

'Knock 'em dead, my superstar baby!' Mum shouted to me, and settled down on the bench under the shelter, scrolling through her phone.

I took a breath and knocked on the door, worried my hands were sweating. What if they wanted to shake my hand

and it was all wet? I was surprised to find that a woman opened the door. She had jet-black hair and massive false eyelashes. She was a lot older than me, maybe thirty or thirty-five.

'You must be Emma,' she said. 'Come in, darling, come in.'

I stepped inside, looking around the shabby hallway. I didn't look back at Mum, but I knew she would be watching. She was probably relieved that a woman answered the door, and they weren't just pervy men.

'I'm Cath,' she said, eyeing me. 'Let me get your coat. You want a drink?'

'Yes, please.' My voice was so quiet. I coughed to get the nerves out and not sound like a stupid kid. They'd asked me to come because they thought I had what it took. And I did. It was time to stop being a little girl about it.

'Come into the kitchen with me.' Cath was really chirpy and super friendly, talking and laughing at nothing in particular. Her eyes were wide and very blue and her pupils were huge, like she was high on something.

The inside of the house was nicer than it had seemed on first impressions. Wood floors and clean white walls, with nice pictures of other girls. They were all pretty. Was I as pretty as them? Would my picture fit in? One picture in the kitchen, bigger than the others, was an arty photo of a woman lying on a pink sofa, completely naked. My cheeks heated up as I realised it was Cath.

She handed me some wine. It was nothing like the wine I'd had before. It was delicious. We stood in the kitchen, me with my wine, while Cath poured herself something else. 'Vodka,' she said with another laugh. 'Less fattening. Do you want some?'

Without waiting for an answer, she poured me a glass of that, too.

'I haven't finished my wine,' I said.

Cath whacked on some music and shouted over it, 'Well, down it then! Don't be boring. Joe was right. Your hair's amazing and you have got the prettiest little face.'

I downed the wine like she told me to, and then took the vodka. I wanted to ask where the guys were but wanted to play it cool.

She read my mind. 'Joe and Zane are on their way.'

She was dancing about, clearly off her head. I laughed and watched her. Then she topped up my vodka. I had a vague thought about my mum, how she might smell it on me when I came back to the bus stop.

Cath was asking me a load of questions. 'So you live around here? Did you get a bus in that hot dress? God, I love Nina Simone, don't you?' She didn't give a second for me to answer. It was like she lost interest the moment she asked.

Then the front door opened and banged shut. Cath stopped dancing and turned down the music. 'All right, babes?' she said as Joe and Zane walked in.

'Well well well!' Joe said. 'Look who it is. Cath, didn't I tell you she was hot?'

'You did, babe.'

My head was spinning a bit. I was giggling at something Cath had said that I'm sure wasn't that funny.

Zane grinned at me and said, 'You look beautiful, darling.' He came over and kissed my cheek.

Joe kissed Cath on the lips. 'We're going to take Emma here upstairs to take some pictures. You OK to stay here, yeah?'

Cath looked at me, then back at Joe. 'You sure you don't want me to come up?'

'No babe, it's cool, you stay down here,' Joe said.

I was kind of relieved. I couldn't quite put my finger on why I didn't want her there. Maybe not wanting to feel like I'd have to live up to whatever she'd already done?

We went upstairs and into a bedroom. There was nothing in there really except a bed, a long mirror against one of the plain white walls, and a couple of camera tripods set up. I pulled my make-up pouch out of my bag and touched up my make-up by the window while they fiddled about with the lights and the cameras. I craned my neck a bit as I looked outside. I could see Mum, still sitting patiently at the bus stop staring at her phone. It was reassuring.

Joe told me to get comfortable on the bed. I'm not sure I was giving off 'comfortable' as I pulled at my dress, but they were both still looking at the cameras, setting them up.

After a few moments, Joe looked up from his camera towards me. 'All right? Ready to get some shots?'

I wasn't really.

Zane said, 'Honestly babe, it's chill. Keep your shoes on and get right up on the bed. Try a couple kneeling . . . or lie down if you want?'

I hesitated, starting to move slowly. Zane jumped up and landed on the bed next to me, making me laugh.

'Come on!' he said with a grin. 'Don't be shy!'

I lay back on the bed and he jumped back up over to where Joe was clicking a few shots.

'That's it, babe, give us a smile,' said Joe.

Click click click. Joe took the pictures and Zane carried on directing me. He got me to turn over and lie down on my belly with my legs kicked up behind me.

'Cath! Get some shoes!' Joe shouted down the stairs after a minute. I blushed. They'd noticed my scruffy high heels.

'What size is she?' Cath shouted up.

Joe looked at me. I showed him five fingers. This was sort of fun.

'Five,' he called, then kept on clicking.

Cath came up with some amazing shoes. Bright red stilettos with heels so high my toes would barely touch the floor in them.

'I won't be able to walk in these,' I said, putting them on.

Cath said, 'They're not for walking in', and winked at me.

I was starting to relax. Joe and Zane seemed happy with what I was doing. With every click of the camera they told me how beautiful I was. My mind wandered to Mum again as they took the pictures. I reckoned she'd be on one of her dating apps, scrolling and swiping, hoping one of those men would get with her, pay a bill or give her a bit of cash. Enjoying myself now, I started to really believe the thing I'd been hoping all this time – that I wasn't going to end up like her. I was really going to have a chance to make something of my life.

'OK, darling, now take your dress off,' Joe said.

I suddenly refocused and was back in the room. 'What?'

'Your dress, babe,' he said, looking down at his camera. 'Take it off.'

I hesitated only a minute longer, but then I did it. I wasn't a kid. This is what they wanted. It would be OK. I lay back on the bed, and they started snapping more photos of me in just my new knickers and bra. I tried to stay relaxed and channel Lizzo. Told myself to be proud of my body.

As Joe clicked away, Zane kept his eyes straight on me. 'Up on your elbows, babe. Lean back, touch your boob a little bit. Beautiful, now put your finger in your mouth and look right into the camera.'

They took loads and loads of pictures. I tried to just go with it all, not overthink things. This was good. This was how I was going to really grab people's attention.

At last, they said they had everything they needed. I got dressed, straightened myself up and bounced out of the house.

It had started to rain, and Mum was huddled under the bus shelter. She sprang up.

'How'd it go?' she said loudly.

'Shhh!' I grabbed her arm to walk away. I didn't want Cath or Zane or Joe to see I'd brought my mum. They'd think I didn't trust them or something, or that I was just some silly kid who wasn't ready for whatever was to come.

'How'd it go?' Mum repeated. She frowned a bit. 'You been drinking?'

I belched gently. 'It went great. And yeah, a bit. Let's just walk.'

Once we were round the corner and headed towards the next bus stop, I squealed, 'MUM! It was amazing! They said I was a natural! And look!' I held up the two crisp fifty-pound notes Zane had just given me.

'Another hundred quid!' Mum exclaimed.

'Yes!' I was jumping up and down, even though it killed my feet in mum's old shoes. 'For the photos they just took! They reckon they can manage my brand on Insta, make me an influencer.'

'That's amazing, darling,' Mum gasped. 'Those girls make so much money!'

'I know! They're gonna create a whole new Instagram page for me with this new lot of pics. Properly promote it.'

They'd liked what I'd done on Insta so far, but they'd promised me so many more followers if they created a new account for me.

This was it. This was how it was going to start. I was *in*. So what if I'd felt a bit uncomfortable about some of the stuff? That was just what you had to do to get ahead in this business. It was all kicking off for me.

*

Zane called me that night. 'You was really good today. Did you see the pictures on the new account?'

Was he joking? Course I had. I checked the views, like, a hundred times a minute. There were loads! The account they'd set up on Insta was @KissingEmma69. The pictures they'd uploaded looked amazing. I could tell they'd put some pretty heavy-duty filters on and probably done a bit of tweaking to the images, but all the girls on Insta accounts like this did that. I actually looked pretty amazing, even if I said so myself. It was like looking at someone else. The woman I'd always wanted to be, maybe. One of the sexier shots had got almost a thousand likes within an hour. And the account already had 1328 new followers. 1328! In one day!

'You're different to other girls, you know, Emma. You've got that classy edge that really sets you apart,' Zane said.

I smiled into the phone, feeling my face flush with the compliment. 'I bet you say that to all the girls,' I said with a laugh.

'Nah, just you.'

I half thought about asking for the login details for the new account so I could upload some vids and other stuff, too, but Zane said he had to go, and I didn't want to rock the boat so soon.

I did send the links to Matilda and Soreya though. We sat scrolling through the pictures while we waited for the first bell at school a day or two later. I was gagging for study leave, for our exams to start properly, so that I didn't have to think about whether I was meant to be turning up at school.

Matilda sucked in a long breath. 'Have you tried googling this lot?' she said. She and Soreya exchanged glances. 'There's no trace of their modelling agency online.'

I shrugged. 'Who cares? I got a hundred quid for just lying around for a couple of hours!' I still couldn't believe it.

'And now there's half-naked pictures of you all over Instagram,' Soreya said, half chuckling. I decided to ignore that.

Matilda was a little bit more supportive. 'There are half-naked pictures of lots of people on Instagram,' she pointed out.

Soreya looked at her phone again. 'I know . . . but Emma's my mate! It's just weird seeing a mate do all this . . .' She mimicked one of my poses which, from her, fully dressed, was hilarious.

'Shut up, I don't pout like that!' I said, laughing. 'I made a point of not pouting like that!'

'Whatever,' she said. 'Look, now you're rich you can take me and Matilda to Iceshack. We'll go and celebrate your new career as a whatever it is, eh?'

We went to Iceshack after school, and for the first time ever I was able to pay for a whole order, for all of us, not just my own drink. I felt a bit bad at spending money I could have given to Mum for saving up, but I reckoned there was plenty more where that had come from.

'This must be what it's like being friends with Taylor Swift.' Soreya giggled.

'Nah, Taylor would've bought us hamburgers too,' Matilda joked, jabbing me in the ribs as she picked up her milkshake.

'You wait till my Insta *really* takes off. I'll get you both hamburgers *and* let you share my chips,' I said. 'But you won't be allowed to touch me, or make eye contact with me, OK?'

'OK,' they both said, deadly seriously.

*

For the time being, I was still doing my Saturday job at the café. After my shift that weekend, I went to see Suze.

She had expanded her café upstairs into what was the living room of the flat. She'd made it into a cute tea room with retro tables and chairs, all deliberately mismatched, like downstairs. She had a cake stand with some amazing cupcakes, and in the downstairs area she'd made room for a little counter so she could make sandwiches.

It was quite busy when I got there, and she quickly made me a coffee while I waited to talk to her. I told her about everything that had happened with Zane and Joe, and she raised an eyebrow at me as she cleared off one of the tables.

'Emma my darling, you and your mother really are sweet and innocent, aren't you?' she said.

I pursed my lips, and showed her my @KissingEmma69 page. I had over three thousand followers now. 'Look! That's just in a few days!'

Suze lowered her glasses and looked at my pictures. 'So you went to the house of a total stranger and let two older men take you into a bedroom and take pictures of you in your undies?'

I frowned. She made it sound different to how it was. 'There was another woman there!' I pointed out, taking my phone back.

Suze shook her head. 'Oh, Emma, it doesn't matter. These people are twice your age and a hundred times more devious.'

It was starting to annoy me how she didn't seem to be on board with the whole thing, even after I told her how much they had paid me.

'That's not very much, darling,' Suze said. 'To you, yes, but you've got to remember it's all relative. You may have a tenner in your pocket and a homeless bloke will consider you loaded. These men sound like creeps to me.'

'Zane and Joe aren't creeps, though. They're agents and photographers, and—'

Suze threw her head back and laughed. 'Photographers? That what they're called these days?'

I crossed my arms. 'Don't be like that, Suze. They said they're going to make me a star, and I believe them. Look what they've done for me already.'

Suze exhaled. 'Young girls like you aren't going to be just so-called clients to men in their thirties. And certainly not girlfriend material. If anything, you're prey. Just don't be alone with either of them, and call me any time if you need to, OK?'

Mum had always drummed into me that we needed money, but now that I was getting there, Suze was starting to make me feel nervous. I didn't want her getting in my head, though. Zane and Joe were all right. I knew they were. I decided it was best to change the subject.

'Looks so nice here now, anyway,' I said breezily. 'Upstairs is brilliant!'

'Yeah,' Suze said, clearing away the coffee cups. She seemed happy to move on, too. 'In fact, I wanted to ask – do you fancy doing some shifts here again? Or are you a full-time gangster's moll now?'

'Ah, you know what? I loved working here but I've got to get two buses to get here, and I need to keep myself free, Zane said, for any last-minute modelling work that'll come in.'

'He said that now, did he?' Suze looked at me. I could tell she was still worried, but it wasn't her style to push a point. 'Just promise me you'll be careful, Emma.'

TWENTY-TWO

The next day, I went to Joe's again.

'We're gonna get creative babe,' he told me almost as soon as I arrived. 'Don't get too comfy, we're heading out.'

Cath was there too, and they both walked over to Joe's car, where Zane was waiting. I followed them and got in. I felt totally safe. Suze didn't know what she was talking about.

We drove out to Horse Hill Wood, and I looked out the window curiously as things got leafier and more rural.

'The light is perfect out here,' Joe said, pulling over into a little clearing in the trees.

'Yeah,' agreed Zane. 'But we got to be quick before it goes.'

They wanted me in my underwear again.

'But it's freezing!' I said. I didn't want to add the other obvious thing – that I wasn't too keen to get down to my knickers in a public place.

Cath waved her hands in the air dismissively. 'It makes for a really great shot, trust me. It'll be quick if you just get on with it.'

'But someone might see . . .' I said, still unsure.

Zane looked irritated. 'Emma, no one will see. We need to hurry, we don't want to lose the light. Besides, you're not on your own – Cath's gonna join in on this one.'

I took a deep breath and shrugged out of my dress quickly. Cath stripped too. She even took her bra off. I wasn't expecting her to be taking pictures with me, let alone getting her boobs out. I tried to act like I was fine with it, but I didn't know where to look.

Zane directed this one. He made Cath lean against a tree with me posing next to her, clicking the camera the whole time and saying, 'Beautiful, gorgeous,' and, 'Emma, put your hands on Cath's hip . . .'

I did as I was told.

'Look into each other's eyes? OK, now both to the camera . . .' He clicked the camera a few more times, then let out a sigh. 'Cath, great, you're super sexy – but Emma, you look stiff. Can you just relax, babe?'

I so badly wanted to get this right. I nodded quickly and tried to let the tension out of my muscles and face.

'Don't be shy, darling,' Cath said. 'This is art. Just enjoy it!'

I did the best I could, though it was cold, and the woodland felt damp, and I was feeling awkward and anything but sexy. Finally, it was all done and Joe and Zane seemed relatively satisfied. Zane handed me a hundred quid again, and they drove me home. I clutched the money right in my hands until I got in the flat, where I unrolled the two fifties and stared at them. A couple of hours' work and all this cash again?

The next morning, I called my cleaning clients, and Mrs Jeenal at the Bunny Park café and said I was quitting. I didn't need any of those piddly jobs now – I was bound for more.

*

That night Zane rang me up. To my surprise, he wanted to go out, just me and him.

'I'll take you for a few drinks yeah? We can talk properly then. Say in an hour or so?'

What did 'drinks' mean? A date? Or was this work? I couldn't wear the same dress I'd been using for the shoots so far, he'd already seen that one. I wasn't sure what to go for, but eventually I put on my smartest jeans and a tight, glittery T-shirt Mum had got me two Christmases ago. Seeing how nervous and excited I was, Becca let me go into her room and use some of her make-up. She had bags and bags of it. She hardly ever wore it herself.

Zane picked me up in his car at eight o' clock. I flew down the stairs to meet him. Catching my reflection in the window of his car, I reckoned I looked eighteen. Maybe even nineteen.

'You look amazing, Emma!' Zane said as I got in the car.

I smiled at him. I had no idea where he was going to take me, but I just sat in the car trying to play it cool, feeling glad that the late spring air was warm enough that it was OK I hadn't worn a coat or cardi.

We stopped outside a snooker hall. 'Just got to pop in here for a sec, babe,' Zane said. 'You wait in the car.'

It was more than a second. I was there for about half an hour, waiting like a lemon. What was he doing?

Eventually Zane came out. He threw an envelope in my lap. 'Hang on to that for me, babe?' he said, then pulled away, driving fast.

The envelope was fat, full, and not stuck down. I had a peek, and actually gasped. It was bulging with fifty-pound notes.

Zane glanced over at me and grinned. 'Just a bit of business.'

'I've never ever seen so much money in my whole life!' I told him.

'Well, then you haven't lived.' He winked at me. 'You'll get your own stack soon enough.'

I raised an eyebrow, even as the thought made a grin spread on my face. 'What kind of business pays like this, though? I thought you were a model scout?'

'Oh, I do a bit of this and a bit of that. You know.'

I decided it was best not to push it.

We eventually stopped at a club quite far out of town. I was a bit nervous about being asked for ID, but we walked straight in. No paying at the door, no queuing. The place was rammed and noisy, and Zane was pressing fifties into everyone's hand – the bouncers, the door staff, the waiters. Fifty pounds like it was nothing!

We were taken to a private booth and Zane bought champagne – *actual* champagne. He handed me a glass, and I could barely speak. It was all so posh, like a film, like nothing I'd ever seen before.

Zane introduced me to loads of different people, mostly blokes, till I was dizzy from the excitement and the bubbles in my drink. There was no way I could remember all those names. I was like a demented parrot just going, 'Hello hello hello hello.' A few girls came up too. They were nice to me, but didn't sit with us. Zane put his arm around me when he talked to his friends, and my heart jumped. This had to mean I was important. All these people wanted to talk to him, and he was letting them know I was his – his client, his . . . I wasn't sure what.

I drank the champagne till I really felt relaxed, like Zane told I would. He smelled nice. His clothes were nice. As he chatted to people, he gently touched me – my arm or my hand, just really lightly – and he'd occasionally look over at me and smile. Eventually, a waitress whispered something in his ear, and Zane took my hand. We followed her to a more private booth, one that had curtains around it.

'Finally,' Zane said to me as we sat down. The waitress put our glasses on the small table and closed the curtains again as she left. 'I've got you all to myself.'

I perched on the red velvet seat, my heart beating fast. I felt shy suddenly. Zane wasn't like the boys at school. He was a man – and someone obviously special. He leaned in and started saying stuff in my ear, telling me I was sexy and beautiful, that we were going to make a load of money together. His hand was on my thigh, and the other hand was touching my shoulder, then my face. I looked up at him and he leaned in . . . and before I knew it, he was kissing me. He tasted sweet, fizzy, like the champagne. He kissed me gently, keeping his hands on my face.

'What are the chances of you coming home with me tonight?' he whispered.

I thought about what Suze had said, about not being alone with him. I thought about what had happened with Mo, and Elliot. I felt drunk, dizzy, but I wanted to get it right this time. 'I trust you,' is what I found myself saying.

Zane laughed, 'Well, that's good to know. Shall we?'

It wasn't until I got outside that I realised how drunk I was. The outside air hit me, and my head started spinning as I tried to put one high-heeled foot in front of the other.

'You're stumbling, babe,' Zane said. 'Not a good look. Come on, I'll look after you.'

He put his arm round me as we walked to his car, and he helped me in, then drove us back into town. His flat was above a shop, and I felt only a little bit less drunk when we got out of the car.

'Do you live on your own?' I asked.

'Yes, my lady. It's just me and you,' he said as he let me in.

I rummaged vaguely in my handbag, trying to make sure my phone was there just in case, but it was like I forgot what I was doing the minute we walked inside. I didn't say a lot once we were in his flat, and neither did he. It was pretty much getting down to it. Sex. Not messing around, no awkwardness even, really. I wished Suze wasn't in the back of my head, telling me I shouldn't be here, I shouldn't be doing this. If I was honest, it wasn't Suze, though. It was me.

Zane rolled off me. At least I was dimly aware of him taking off a condom. He reached for his phone, and I saw on his screen that it was one o'clock in the morning. Shit. Mum was going to wonder where I was.

'What's your postcode?' Zane asked.

I told him. I didn't register what he was doing as he tapped on his phone. I was still drunk, tired and we'd just had sex, which I sort of hadn't expected to happen.

'Get dressed,' he said. 'Your Uber's here in three minutes.'

He was already up, pulling on his clothes, straightening himself out. Even in my foggy brain, I'd thought about telling Mum I'd stayed the night at Matilda's or something. Why was he rushing me off?

'Have I done something wrong?' I couldn't help asking as I put my clothes back on.

He leaned down and kissed my head. 'I've just got some business back at the club.' He was going all the way back there? 'I'll come down with you, make sure you get in safe.'

That was it. The next minute, I was in a cold cab on my own, going home.

*

I stayed in bed in Nan's living room late into the next morning. Mum came in with a cuppa for me. When I'd got in, I'd vaguely noted that she was still out too, so at least I hadn't needed to explain myself. I'd pretended to be snoring when she finally stumbled in an hour after I had.

'Fun night, sleepyhead?' she said as she put the tea down.

I didn't want to tell her about my night with Zane, or how it had ended. I was embarrassed. He'd practically booted me out once we'd had sex. I did mutter something about him taking me out to meet some people.

'It was nice, Mum. He was nice. I came home though. I didn't want you to worry.'

Mum frowned. 'You didn't upset him did you, darling? Do anything silly?'

'No! I was fine, everything was fine. I'm just tired.'

I kind of thought I might have done something wrong, though. Otherwise why had he rushed me out? Why did I keep messing up with guys?

I texted Zane later that day. Four times in the end. He never wrote back.

'Stop texting him,' Mum said, noticing my phone sat in my lap. 'Men don't like it when you're needy.'

Why this again? Why wasn't it normal to want to speak to someone who'd actually been inside your body the day before?

I sucked in a breath. 'Mum . . . What if he doesn't want me to work for him any more? What if I've messed that up?'

'Oh god, Emma, surely not!' said Mum. 'You've got almost four thousand followers on that Instagram thingy now. Surely that means he wants to give you more work?'

I stared at my phone again. 'I don't know. I just wish he'd call back.'

I needed to know where I stood with Zane – with work as well as personally. I needed answers, and I remembered where he lived. So I got the bus there.

I was shaking as I walked up to the door. He'd think I was mental, a stalker, but we'd done all those things in bed, things I'd never done before, and he'd told me I was beautiful over and over again. How could it be OK to do all those things with someone, get naked with them, have sex, but then not OK if you texted them or knocked on their door?

I rang the bell. He didn't answer. I rang again. I'd come all the way there, so figured I might as well try to see him.

Eventually his head popped out the upstairs window. He had no top on.

'Emma. Christ!' He disappeared and after a minute, the door opened. He was in his dressing gown. 'What is it?' He didn't seem angry, but there was an edge, like he might *get* angry if I didn't say things right. 'What is it?' he repeated.

Suddenly my mouth was like sandpaper. I couldn't speak. Eventually I heard myself say, 'I-I wanted to know if everything was all right?'

He sighed. 'Everything is all right, Emma. Look, I can't talk now. I'll text you when to come back.'

I nodded mutely. He shut the door.

I thought about going back home, but what if he texted me and I wasn't nearby? So I walked along to a park and sat on a bench, staring at my phone. Why hadn't he just let me in? Was there another girl there?

An hour passed. I started to feel more and more embarrassed and stupid. I was an idiot. The guy didn't answer a few texts and I just turned up at his house? I started to think that maybe I should go home.

I scrolled down all the messages I'd had from Matilda and Soreya over the last week or so. I'd barely returned any of them, and if I had, it was just with an emoji or a GIF, so they wouldn't think I was ghosting them. Most of their messages were about our exams and school and asking where I was. I didn't know what to say to them. It was like in an instant, I was living in a different world.

My phone beeped.

Come over

Zane had dressed when I got there. His music was on loud, but he turned it down a bit as I sat down. It was strange being back in his flat. It had seemed so nice the night before, everything had looked good, but now the place looked dingy.

'No man likes being pestered, Emma,' he said. He looked at me. Cold.

'I-I know,' I stammered. 'I know. I just thought I might have done or said something to piss you off. I needed to know, what with working with you and that . . .'

'Working with me?' Zane didn't smile. He came up close and glared down at me. 'Emma, you don't work with me, you work *for* me. Understood?'

I nodded, avoiding his eyes. He lit a cigarette and blew smoke out of the open window.

'I don't know, Emma,' he said. 'You're beautiful, you've got a great body, you were fun when we went out. I did think,

"Yeah! She might be my girl." But when we came back here, I thought the sex would be really good, but . . .'

Oh my god. There was something wrong with the way I had sex?

'But when we got to it you was . . . boring. Vanilla.'

I risked glancing at him. 'What? What do you mean?'

'You were vanilla. Ordinary, you know? I thought it would be different, young woman your age.' He came over to me, his voice softening a bit. 'But we can work on it, OK? Loosen you up a bit. I'll show you some stuff that properly turns men on.'

I swallowed. 'OK,' I said. I couldn't risk messing things up again.

He leaned down and started kissing me.

I stayed the night with him this time.

*

The next day when I got back to the flat, Mum and Nan were in the kitchen. As soon as I walked in, I could tell Mum had been crying.

'It was only meant to be till you were on your feet,' Nan was saying. 'And I'll be honest with you, darling, I'd quite like my front room back.' Then she saw me. 'Look what the cat dragged in! Where've you been?'

'Leave her alone,' Mum snapped, reaching out to squeeze my hand. 'You all right, love?'

I nodded. 'Everything's OK now, I think.'

'Good,' she said. 'Good. Because this time your nan is serious, it seems.' She was looking at Nan as she spoke. 'Apparently we have to go.'

Nan went to say something, but Mum stopped her. 'No. Mum, it's all right. I get it. There's no point arguing about it any more. Now is as good a time as any.'

Nan fussed with a cup by the sink, then raised her hands in the air in a shrug.

I couldn't lie – part of me was glad that we had a reason to finally get out of Nan's place. But when we were alone in the front room packing our things, I had to ask the obvious question. 'Mum, where are we actually going to go?'

Mum swiped more tears from her cheeks. 'I don't know, Emma. I just don't know.'

'What about Suze?'

'I can't go calling her,' she said, and laughed even as more tears sprang to her eyes. 'It's embarrassing. I'll just cry.'

I shook my head and fished my phone out of my pocket.

'Come straight over,' Suze said immediately. 'You two always have a home with me, you know that. It's cramped, mind you. I hope you haven't got too much stuff.'

I couldn't help a soft laugh. 'Oh yeah, we'll have a job fitting the contents of our walk-in wardrobe into your place.'

An hour and a half later, having carted all our stuff on the bus, Mum and I were dumping our bags in Suze's spare room. It was small, with a bed that barely counted as a double. We'd have to squash in together to sleep, but we'd done it before, and at least it was a room of our own. Still, with all of our things packed in with us, you could hardly see the floor.

'Give us a couple of your bags,' Suze suggested. 'We'll clear space in a cupboard in my room and you can leave some of your kit in there.'

I felt a sense of calm settle over me as Mum, Suze and I sat down to takeaway pizza in the closed café. Maybe, just maybe, things would finally be OK.

TWENTY-THREE

A day or two later, I was back at Joe's. And again, he wanted me in my underwear.

'Babe,' he said to me. 'We need more photos and videos in the bag for Insta stories.'

Zane was there. All the stuff with Zane a couple of nights ago was still whirling about in my head, but I never said anything about it, just tried to remain cool and calm. So during a break while Joe went off to find another memory card for his camera, I told Zane what had happened with Nan asking us to move out. To my surprise, he immediately perked up.

'You can't live like that, Emma,' he said to me, suddenly friendlier. 'You ought to pack up a bag and come and stay with me.'

'Really?'

'Yeah, really.' He kissed me. 'You're my investment.' He

grinned, holding my hand and kissing my knuckles too. 'I got to protect my investment, don't I? I want you to move in with me, then I can really keep an eye on you.'

As much as I had enjoyed the couple of nights we'd spent at Suze's, the idea of having all of Zane's attention was massively appealing. Asking me to move in meant he cared, right?

As soon as we were done with the pictures, Zane insisted on driving me round to Suze's to pick up my stuff. When we walked in and I explained that I'd be going to stay with him for a bit, Suze gave him evils. Wouldn't shake his hand. While Mum stayed downstairs making small talk with Zane, Suze came with me when I went to pack. She pointedly gave me a smaller suitcase than the one I'd come with.

'Emma love, you sure about this?' she said. 'About him?'

'He's lovely, Suze, honestly,' I assured her. 'He looks after me.'

She narrowed her eyes. 'How long have you known him?'

I rolled my eyes. 'OK, not long, but he's a good guy. I know he is. Don't worry.'

'I can see where Emma gets her graceful nature from,' Zane was telling Mum as me and Suze came back downstairs. Mum was smitten.

'You've landed on your feet there, love,' she whispered to me as I hugged her goodbye. 'I know this young man will take care of you.' Her eyes glittered as she glanced at Zane. 'Keep him sweet, all right? This could be good for us.'

I squeezed her into another hug before she let me go. This was the first time we'd be living separately.

'We're still gonna find a flat, you and me. This is just temporary,' I blurted to Mum.

She nodded. 'And in the meantime, make the most of this, sweetheart.'

*

Back at his flat, Zane pointed at a little chest of drawers. 'You can put your stuff in there.' He rummaged around in his wardrobe and pulled out an empty shoe box. 'And put your make-up or whatever in here. Don't clutter up the bathroom with that stuff. I don't like it. Keep it all together, yeah?'

Did he want me here or not? 'Course,' I said moodily. 'Like my mum said, this is only temporary.'

'What do you mean?'

'I mean, we'll get a flat together still, once we've saved some more money.'

He laughed and shook his head. 'You wanna cut that mummy cord, Emma.'

I frowned. 'Why would I do that?'

'Mummy wants you to be her little girl for ever,' Zane said. 'But you're to be *my* girl now. I say what's temporary and what's not.'

I stayed quiet and packed away my clothes. I got the vibe that if I said one more thing, he'd get annoyed with me, so I decided it was best to leave it for now.

*

It was finally happening. People were sending me things – underwear and make-up – at Joe's address, wanting me to use it and tag them on the Instagram page, like proper influencer stuff. I'd have preferred money, to be honest. But Joe and Zane promised me that more of that would come, we just had to keep working hard and being patient.

Zane was out most days, and if he'd been out all night he'd sleep all day, so I never saw him much in daylight. He didn't come with me to do the photos at Joe's any more. I'd go to school from time to time. Because we were heading into study leave, it wasn't so noticeable that I was away so much. Lots of days I'd go to Joe's and put on the new underwear and make-up that had been sent. They needed it to be shared ASAP to get the proper endorsements. I'd pose, Joe would post the pictures up after doing his filtering and stuff, and then I'd wait for the likes and comments to come flooding in. Then he'd put me in a cab home in time for Zane to wake up.

A couple of weeks after I moved in with Zane, I learned from Matilda and Soreya that Suze had turned up at school with Mum. I called, angry that they'd gone behind my back.

'Mum, what were you playing at?' I demanded.

I heard her sigh on the other end of the phone. 'It was Suze's idea, sweetheart.'

Suze's voice grew louder in the background as she took the phone off Mum. 'I needed to make some things clear to the school, Em,' she said. 'They've been ringing your mum, talking all threatening. I'm still a social worker at heart, babe.'

Turned out Suze had managed to talk to Mrs Sharma to explain my circumstances, and between them they'd agreed to let me try and catch up on coursework online and sit my exams.

'You won't forgive yourself if you don't even try,' Suze told me. 'Fail them all, who cares? But turn up.'

She had a point. I definitely wanted to do Drama at least, and I reckoned I could pass a few of the others without having to try too hard. So while Zane was out, and when I wasn't shooting, I did what I could to catch up. I hung around the flat a lot, so it gave me uninterrupted quiet time. Zane didn't like me going out on my own, unless it was to Joe's. When it came to exams, if he was about, I actually had to persuade him to let me go to school and sit my GCSEs.

Soreya and Matilda didn't really ask much about where I'd been or what was going on with Zane and Joe and my modelling and all that. They hardly ever even liked the Instagram posts, I'd noticed. They were totally focused on the exams.

'I've literally not left my room for weeks except to eat or pee,' Soreya said.

There was no time to chat after the English exam that day. All they wanted to talk about was what had been on the paper, and then they rushed home to revise for the next one. It seemed a bit keen, to be honest. I'd hoped to spend a bit of time with them while I had a window.

'Saddos, innit,' Zane said when he picked me up in his car afterwards. I'd asked him to come and get me, seeing as I hadn't been able to catch up with my friends. 'I got plans for you, babe. You don't need exams and all that shit. Me and Joe have a bit of news.'

A company called Sun Cowgirl had offered them two thousand pounds for me to wear their clothes and post the pictures on Insta! I had almost ten thousand followers now. I'd get comments from girls like 'You're so pretty!' and 'You're an inspiration' – as well as pervy comments from guys, of course. But like Joe and Zane told me to, I replied to the girls, making sure I liked each and every nice comment. They were the ones who'd buy the stuff I was being asked to promote, so they said that was really important.

'It makes people feel connected to you,' Joe said. 'You got to build that connection and they'll buy anything off you.'

The Sun Cowgirl clothes were super skimpy bikinis. Joe eagerly laid them all out, and I put them on for him to take the pictures. He put them up on Instagram almost straight away, and then handed me £200 in cash. I was pleased to get double what I usually got after a shoot, but I couldn't help wondering about the rest. After all, Zane had said the clothing company was paying two grand for me to wear that stuff.

Back at the flat, I tried asking Zane about it when he was relaxed, drinking a beer in the kitchen.

'Ten per cent, baby,' he said. 'Me and Joe are investing a lot of our time in you, and time is money, you got that?'

I nodded, and drew a breath. 'But . . . I'm the one wearing the clothes, right? It's me they're paying for. Two hundred quid doesn't really seem fair.'

He went quiet for a minute. 'How much rent you paying here, Emma?' He did that thing where he stood close, towered over me and glared down at me. He was so close I had to take a step back. He backed me against the wall. Not pushing me, but sort of just forcing me back with his energy. 'Go on then, how much?'

'None,' I said. 'Please don't get angry—'

'No, we obviously need to clear a few things up. What do you pay in bills?'

'OK, I get your point. Please.'

'And who buys your food, your clothes? Taxis?'

'You do,' I said.

'That's right, Emma. Keep that in your head, yeah?' He tapped my forehead with one finger, his eyes drilling into me, then backed off, sipping out of his beer bottle again. 'Don't give me that unfair shit again.'

*

A couple of weeks later, all my exams were done, and I found a chance to go round and see Suze. She wanted me to help out in her café on Saturdays.

'Go on, Emma, it's been so busy here,' she said. 'It'll be lovely for your mum, too. She hardly gets to see you these days.'

'I'll think about it, Suze, I promise,' I told her.

I wanted to – it was just getting Zane to agree to it. So I waited for a day he was in a good mood, when he'd slept and had a wallet full of cash again.

'So . . .' I said casually. 'I'm thinking of working at Suze's café on Saturdays, to help her out a bit, you know. You OK with that?'

'You don't need a job, babe, you got me. I'm your full-time job,' he said.

'Yeah, but you're never really here at the weekends anyway, and I would see my mum and Suze and get a bit of extra cash, maybe—'

He didn't hurt me, not really. But in a flash he'd pushed me up against the wall, knocking the lamp over. For a second I thought he was going to hit me, but he just hissed in my face, 'No girl of mine works in a shitty little café run by a bitch like that.' He grabbed my arm and yanked me across the room, smashing me into the cupboard. 'And clean up that crap all over the top of the dresser. What did I tell you about leaving your shit everywhere?' Then he left the room and slammed the door behind him.

When I heard him leave the flat, the feeling of relief reminded me of how it had been with Dad. I stared at myself in the mirror. I was back there again. Just like Mum. There was a bit of blood on my eyebrow where I'd hit the cupboard, but apart from that I was all right.

On the outside at least.

A moment later, I heard him come back again. He walked into the bedroom.

'Oh, babe, babe, I'm sorry . . .' He knelt in front of me and hugged me. I started crying. 'God, I'm so sorry, I didn't mean to hurt you. Please, please say you forgive me?' He held my face in his hands and kissed it all over. 'Do you forgive me, Emma? That is never going to happen again.'

I thought he was going to cry. 'It's OK, it's OK,' I told him and we held each other for a bit. Then we had sex – nice sex, gentle sex, vanilla sex. I really did forgive him. He was nothing like my dad.

We didn't say any more about me working in Suze's café, though. Life carried on with Zane getting up at about one o'clock in the afternoon, going off to do business then coming back and taking me to the club or the snooker hall with him, where I had learned to be friendly to his mates but not too friendly, and look nice but not like a tart, and make sure I was there next to him at any moment when he turned to look. I had to ask him when I needed the toilet and stuff like that.

But he loved me, that was the important thing. He told me so every day.

My Instagram page was doing really well now. Zane and Joe took pictures that were different to the other girls', and sometimes I made little videos of myself dancing and lip-syncing to whatever song was high in the charts. They were quirky and quite funny, while looking totally hot, of course. My followers rose so high, soon we were closing in on thirty thousand. Zane was well pleased.

Mum started coming over and doing my hair and make-up for my posts, and Zane was fine about it because she did it so well. The pictures were way better when she was involved, they couldn't deny it. Best of all, it meant I got to see her more. She put bronzer all over me and covered every bit of blotchy skin, even the weird stretch marks I had on my back.

Mum still had a couple of her cleaning jobs, and she helped Suze in the café. She told me funny things that happened there, things Suze had said, and made me miss being with the two of them.

'Why don't you come over?' she asked one day while she was finishing off my make-up. 'Just for a bun and a cuppa.'

'He doesn't like it, Mum,' I whispered, hoping Zane couldn't hear. He'd decided to come with me to Joe's that day.

Mum looked at me for a moment. 'Is he good to you, Emma?'

I couldn't tell her the things that had happened, about his temper. I didn't want her to worry. She was so impressed by his car and his clothes and him owning his flat, and the fact that he bought me so many nice things. That he was giving me money and taking care of me.

'Course he is,' I said and changed the subject, showing her some of the dresses he'd bought me.

*

I'd lived with Zane for six weeks now. I knew most of his mates and was a million times more confident than that first time we went out. One night, after a night out, he said, 'I saw you talking to Isla.'

Isla was a girl we always saw at the club.

'Yeah, she was cool.' Was that the right thing to say? Isla

was more my age, at least. I spent a lot of time at the club sitting around with her while the boys talked, just smiling or laughing at their jokes.

'She's hot, right?' he said.

I wasn't really sure why he was bringing it up. Was he trying to make me jealous? 'Yeah, she is,' I agreed, trying not to pout.

He went out without me that night. When he came back, I was shocked to hear a woman's voice. Isla was with him.

'What's going on?' I said to him under my breath while she wandered over to check out the view of the road from the living room window.

'That's not polite, babe,' Zane said. He smelt of booze. 'We've got a guest.'

Isla looked over at me, and I smiled awkwardly.

Zane said, 'What do we say to guests, Emma? We say, "Would you like a drink?"'

'Oh, sorry.' I cleared my throat. It wasn't lost on me that he hadn't answered my question. 'Would you like a drink?'

Isla nodded.

'Get us all a drink, babe,' Zane said. 'Isla, make yourself at home.' He flopped down on to the sofa. Then he pulled Isla down next to him, and kissed her. Right in front of me. I just stood there in shock.

'Drinks, Emma.'

Like a zombie, I walked out of the room. In the kitchen, I got a bottle of vodka and some glasses. I stumbled back to the living room and poured some out, handing a glass to each of them. I gulped mine down in one.

Zane poured me some more. Then he took my hand, pulling me to sit on the other side of him. 'You are so beautiful, babe,' he murmured at me. 'You're doing so well. I'm so proud of you.'

He kissed me, and we all drank some more.

'Do you know how much I love Emma?' Zane told Isla. 'This girl has changed my whole life.'

Isla smiled. 'That's nice, that's really sweet.' She was slurring a bit.

'It's been my ultimate fantasy, Emma, to see you with another girl,' Zane whispered. 'You think Isla's hot, right?'

I didn't answer, staring at my lap.

'Isla is HOT! Isn't she?' he repeated, quite forcefully, into my face.

'Yes, yes, Isla's hot,' I said quickly.

Isla looked at me. 'Babe, if you don't wanna, it's—'

'Of course she wants to,' Zane interrupted.

'I don't,' I said.

It just came out. There was this long pause where no one said a word. I could feel Zane had tensed up.

'I still get paid though, right?' Isla asked.

What did she mean by that?

Zane stood up and pulled me out of the room, saying, 'Excuse us for a second, Isla.'

I was terrified he was angry with me, or what he might do, but he took me through to the bedroom and said, 'Emma, do you have any idea how much money we can make if we take pictures of you and Isla together?'

It was embarrassing, but I was relieved that this was more about business, even if he had kissed Isla in front of me. 'Like I did with Cath?'

'Yeah, but better,' said Zane. 'No disrespect to Cath, but she's a bit past her sell-by date, you know what I mean? But two girls as young and gorgeous as you and Isla, looking like a couple? We'd make so much money on endorsements and all that.'

Tears welled in my eyes. I blinked them away.

'It's just acting. You love acting,' Zane went on. 'You're always on about that. And Isla is totally up for it.'

So we did it.

I pretended Isla was my girlfriend or something, and we took pictures on the sofa together . . . and in bed together, too. I lent her some of the fancy underwear I'd been sent. With the lighting Zane had set up, the pictures looked pretty sexy.

Zane insisted on putting them online straight away, and the likes and extra followers came in the hundreds almost right before our eyes. I stared at the pictures while Zane peeled off notes from a roll in his pocket and handed them to Isla. She got her stuff straight away after that, chucking a quick nod my way before she left.

I wasn't sure if I'd just crossed a line, but it was too late to turn back now.

TWENTY-FOUR

So are u gay now? came the text from Matilda, with a winky face.

I smiled. I could hear her jokey, sarcastic tone even in a text.

I had so many followers now, I didn't always notice people from school following me. But of course they all did, including my friends. Zane had told me never to engage on a personal level on Insta, though – he said to always keep it professional. It all felt totally distant, to be honest. Like that girl on the account with thousands of followers wasn't me, but someone else completely. I suppose she was, in a lot of ways.

'You get packages here every day, you know,' Joe told me.

We had gone to his to take pictures in his studio. Zane was with me. He'd been taking more interest again, especially after the pictures with Isla blew up.

This time, Zane asked me to take my bra off.

'You're gonna get a lot of fans from this,' he said with a grin.

I was about to protest, but then I remembered something. 'You're not allowed nudity on Instagram,' I said hesitantly.

Zane grinned again, even wider this time. 'We'll just tease this on your Insta . . . but the pictures themselves will be for the JustFans account we're setting up for you. That's where the real dough is.'

JustFans had all the sexier pictures, custom nude stuff and things like that. I didn't know how I felt about Joe and Zane setting up a JustFans account for me, to be honest. I'd already had some people under my Instagram posts saying I was a slag for getting my tits out, and that was with my underwear on.

There were some other girls sticking up for me, though. Cath was in charge of writing my more serious posts, and she'd written one as me, saying how I chose to express my femininity was my own business. That one had made it into the *Daily Mail*! I sort of agreed, but I also wasn't ready to be a topless girl on the internet. I tried to focus on the money. Zane was right. One thing I *had* heard about JustFans was how much the people on there made.

'You're getting famous, girl!' Zane continued. 'You saw that little bit in the paper – *Social Media Star Emma Hamilton Shuts Down Criticism of Skimpy Attire*? The JustFans account is the next step. You trust me, don't you?'

Before I knew it, a practically nude photoshoot was underway. He let me see some of the pictures, and I had to admit I did look good. Anyway, once I'd committed, it was just another thing there was no turning back from.

In the weeks that followed, Zane was over the moon about how much money started to come in. Subscribers to the JustFans page were in the hundreds when he let me glimpse it (he told me it was best he controlled the page for business reasons). They all paid a hundred pounds a time to see the pictures they posted of me with no top on. And lingerie companies, make-up and cosmetics companies, a scented candle business and a vitamin drinks company all sent me stuff to post online and all paid one or two grand.

Now Zane and Joe agreed to give me twenty-five per cent of what they told me we were making. I was getting around £500 a week. I'd never seen so much money. I gave half to Mum. But when she mentioned getting our own place, I wasn't sure. Zane was really happy with me now, and I loved the attention. I wasn't ready to give that up to move back in with Mum. She was enjoying living with Suze, wasn't she? I was just glad I could help out.

'I want you to really work it harder, Emma,' Zane told me a few weeks after the first nude shoot. 'You're not a kid, you're a woman. I want you to really trust your powers.'

He'd bought me some really expensive, revealing clothes to wear when he took me out, which he was doing more and more. He was all over me these days, treating me like a queen.

'You're a star, Emma, and it's time you really looked and acted the part. The same old club isn't good enough for you any more. I'm going to take you out to some really classy places and introduce you to some very powerful men, so we need you looking the part, eh?'

We went to a hotel bar in central London, a really exclusive place, Zane said.

'I'm going to introduce you to some friends of mine, associates. They're all millionaires, Emma, in London on business from overseas. Can you handle it?'

I knew it mattered to him to have a pretty girl on his arm – to have *me* on his arm – and I wasn't going to let him down. 'Of course I can,' I said.

Zane smiled. 'Now, you be nice to these guys and babe, I swear, it'll pay back big.'

I thought he meant I had to be charming and chatty so they'd be more impressed with him and do whatever business deal he wanted. He and Joe wanted to get funding for the film they were always talking about making.

There were three much older men waiting for us in the hotel bar, in their fifties or sixties, all in expensive suits and lots of aftershave: two Americans and one Dutch guy. They shook Zane's hand and were all so polite, making sure I was comfortable and ordering me drinks.

'Would you like some food, Emma?' asked one of the Americans. His name was Basil, and he was huge.

'I'm all right, thanks,' I told him, and then carried on drinking and chatting with them. I felt confident and sexy, with Zane and all their attention on me.

I thought Zane was really pleased. He paid me so many compliments in front of those businessmen. He was like, 'Come on, you haven't seen a more beautiful girl in London, have you? Any of you?'

They all agreed that they hadn't.

He got me to tell them about myself. 'She's very adventurous, up for anything and everything,' he said, winking at me.

I laughed, a bit confused. 'Not sure what you mean by that . . .'

'Ah, Emma,' he said, pulling me to him. 'She acts all shy, doesn't she?'

Then he kissed my head, like he was proud of me.

*

A few days later, after Zane had taken me shopping and to a really nice restaurant for lunch, he mentioned those men to me again.

'Babe, you remember that guy Basil we met the other night?' he asked casually.

'Yeah?' I said, eating my fruit salad.

Since I'd moved in with Zane, I was only allowed fruit as a pudding. I never ate any chocolates or cakes at home either. 'You need to look after yourself, babe,' he'd said. 'We can't make you a star if you're a fatty.' He'd been looking at some pictures I'd taken with Cath.

I went, 'Oi! I'm not as skinny as Cath because I actually eat. I'm curvy. What's wrong with that?'

'Nothing, babe,' he told me. 'I think you're beautiful. I'm just saying you're on the cusp, that's all.'

After that I was always worried I looked fat in pictures.

Zane watched me as I speared a pineapple piece. 'That Basil took quite a shine to you. Called me today, asked if he could see you.'

I didn't get it. 'See me? What for?'

'Well, it's like I said. He's in town for a few days and he wants to get away from all the stuffy blokes he works with and have some fun with someone exciting and beautiful. Someone like you.'

My heart sank. 'Right. So . . . what do I have to do?'

Zane shrugged. 'Just be nice. Have some dinner, laugh at his jokes and—' He stopped for a moment, then reached over and held my hand and my gaze. 'And if it comes to it, go back to his hotel and make sure he has a good time. It'll mean good business for me, babe, OK?'

I stared down at my hand in his. Part of me couldn't believe what he was asking, but I knew that look of his. I didn't want to make him angry. Things had been so good with us lately, and if nothing else, he hated me messing up his money.

'What if I can't do it?' I said.

'Can't do what? Get a heap of cash to spend on whatever you want?' His grip was tighter now. 'Babe, he's a sophisticated man who travels all over the world. He only hangs out with the most beautiful women – and in England, Emma, that's you. You ought to be flattered.'

He pulled his chair next to mine and put his arm around me. 'Do you want a life with me, Emma? Are we a team? Are we gonna have everything we ever wanted? Do we both want that? Look at me.'

I looked at him. 'Y-yes,' I stammered.

He kissed me then, and said, 'Then do this thing for me. For us. Just think of it as work. It's a bit of work, that's all.'

*

The next evening, I found myself sat in the bar of the Milestone Hotel. It seemed there was no dinner with Basil once I'd agreed. Just the meeting at his hotel. Which was sort of fine by me, because the quicker this was done the better. I didn't need all the small talk dragging it out any longer than it had to.

Zane had dropped me off and told me to wait in the bar until he messaged me a room number. I was to go to the room, spend an hour with Basil and then return to Zane, who said he'd stay parked across the road, waiting for me.

I sat there perched on a stool with my hair all done, in a tiny, tight red dress and high-heeled shoes. I sipped my Coke, feeling like my heart was going to explode out of my chest. Could everyone tell what I was going to do?

I jumped when my phone buzzed with a message from Zane.

Room 607

My mouth was dry. I stood up, draining my drink. Now I was worried my lipstick had smudged. I walked through the lobby to the massive golden lifts, which had a big mirror next to them. My eyes looked wide and frightened as I checked my reflection.

A porter came past me with a trolley and I jumped again. 'Can I call the lift for you, madam?' he asked.

He must have seen me just standing there staring at the button. I nodded, and he pressed the button for me.

Too soon, it came and the doors opened. I stepped in and tugged the hem of my dress down, suddenly self-conscious with my legs so bare and so much of my cleavage showing.

'Which floor, madam?' asked the porter, stepping in with me.

'I don't know.' I couldn't help worrying the porter knew what I was doing there.

'What room number?'

'607.' Oh god, there was no way he wouldn't guess what I was up to.

The porter's face stayed still and polite. 'That's the sixth floor,' he said. And he pressed the button.

A blindfolded snail would have beaten that lift to the sixth floor. Every second was torture. The porter and I stood there, staring straight ahead as we inched our way up soundlessly. I felt sweaty. I needed air. Finally at the sixth floor, the door opened and I stepped out.

'Have a good evening, madam,' said the porter.

The rooms stretched down endless hallways. I didn't know which one led to 607. I went down the wrong one, turned back and went down another, before I noticed the sequence of numbers were on a little sign at the end of each corridor.

I walked slowly down the right hallway. I got to 600 – and stopped. Between room 600 and 601 was a fire escape door. I stared at it for a few seconds. Room 607 – and whatever Basil wanted to do to me, to pay Zane for – was just a few steps away.

I hesitated a moment longer, then pushed open the fire escape door.

The staircase here was different to the rest of the hotel. Cold and concrete, offering me a route back to the real world. Without another second's thought, I took off my heels and ran down the stairs, all the way, fast, feeling a rush of both relief and fear. The door at the bottom led outside, to the back of the hotel. I ran, still barefoot, in the opposite direction to the main road where Zane was waiting in his car.

Basil would tell Zane I never turned up. Zane would be so angry with me. I had to get off the streets before he started driving around, trying to find me.

I didn't have a plan. I just knew I did not want to go to room 607, and I couldn't go back to Zane's. As I ran, I turned off my phone. I had no money on me, none of my stuff.

What was I going to do?

TWENTY-FIVE

I passed a small hotel, not huge like the ones on the main street. It still looked really posh, though. Safe. So I ran in. Then I stood for a moment, my heart racing so much that I felt giddy. It was only when I felt the carpet under my feet that I remembered I'd taken off my shoes.

A man came over to me, looking concerned. 'Are you all right? You look a bit flushed. I mean, you look beautiful, but flushed.' He spoke very posh and was a little drunk, that was clear. But he didn't seem like a creep.

'I'm OK now,' I said. 'I've just run away from someone.' I laughed a bit hysterically.

'Good for you,' he said. 'And good for me. My name's Con, short for Cornelius. May I know your name?'

He really was the poshest bloke I'd ever met. I smiled at him. 'Emma.'

'Emma,' he said. He took my hand and kissed it. 'Enchanted. May I buy you a drink?'

I needed one, my heart was jumping that fast in my chest. So I nodded, and followed him to the bar.

Cornelius was a name for a ninety-three-year-old bloke living in Victorian times. But this Cornelius was in his twenties – a good-looking guy with glossy blond hair that swept back and down to just above his shoulders, and wide blue eyes.

He bought a bottle of champagne, and I raised my eyebrows as the bartender quietly told him how much it would be.

'You don't have to drink the entire bottle,' Con told me. 'You'd be most welcome to, but it's not compulsory.'

The barman poured us a glass each. 'Shall I bring it over to your table, sir?' he said.

'I'm here with friends,' Con told me, pointing to a group of guys who, like him, seemed to be in their twenties and dressed in casual but clearly expensive clothes. 'Old school buddies of mine. If you prefer, we can get a booth on our own and . . . I don't know, chat?'

'Yeah,' I said. 'Let's do that.'

I was not in the mood to be surrounded by guys. I tried not to think of Zane, of what I'd done and how angry he'd be. I tried not to think about whether I'd screwed up making a living for myself.

'Splendid! That is the correct answer,' Con said, smiling as he nodded to the waiter.

He led me to a booth away from his friends, who looked over at us, raised their glasses, but then just got on with their night.

'Great bunch,' Con said, settling in at our booth. 'But when I saw you rush in like that looking like an utterly stunning but frightened rabbit, I thought, there's a girl with a story.' He smiled at me. 'So, what *is* your story?'

I didn't tell him much. 'I've . . . I've just had a bad night with a bad guy, and I'm interested in forgetting about it for a while,' I said.

'Perfect!' he said. 'Then I'll do the talking if you like, and you can chip in with your own thoughts or to take the piss out of me any time you like. Deal?'

He told me all about his family. His grandad had invented the toaster or something. Well, maybe he hadn't invented it, but he'd started a famous toaster brand, and even though he'd died ages ago, the family still apparently got stacks of money from the toaster company.

'It's not just toasters, mind you,' Con told me. 'We've expanded to fridges, freezers, vacuum cleaners . . . Stop me if my household appliances chat is turning you on too much.'

I said, 'I want you to say "dishwasher" again, but slowly.'

He laughed. He was pretty tuned in, this Con. I liked him. He went quiet for a minute, then said, 'Now, if I'm going to be your knight in shining armour this evening, Emma – which, by the way, I'm very happy to be – you need to tell me a *little* about your story and who you are running away from.'

He seemed sincere, and right in that moment, for the first time in a long while, I felt like I was with a friend. So I caved in and told him everything. About having been scouted by Zane and Joe, about how things had escalated to this evening – about Basil, about the stupid situation I was in.

'So you're a working girl, shall we say?' Con asked, without sounding like he was judging me.

'No, I'm not! I couldn't go through with it, I told you!' I suddenly felt like I was going to cry. 'For ages, Zane made me feel like I could only have him in my life, you know? He said we were a team. But it wasn't him being told to have sex with some old man called Basil, was it?'

Con's eyebrows knitted together sympathetically. 'Christ, imagine! Now, are all stupid names repulsive for you, or just the herb-based ones? Are stupid Latin ones OK?'

I chuckled. 'I think Cornelius is a great name.'

'And *I* think you are impossibly beautiful and lovely. Do you want to come and meet my friends? I've been in Hong Kong for a couple of years and this is the first time I've caught up with them. I'd love to go back for a bit and introduce you.'

'Oh, but I look a mess,' I said. 'I've been crying. My make-up must be all over the place . . .'

'You look perfect.' He took a slow breath. 'But I have a room here. If you like, we can go up there and you can freshen up? Or just have some space?' He stood up and held his hand out. 'What do you say?'

I took his hand. We walked to the lift.

The moment the doors slid shut, Con kissed me. He pulled me to him and put his lips on mine. I was surprised, but only for a second. He gave me deep, sexy kisses that were actually really amazing – the kind when you know a guy really wants you there. I hadn't been kissed like that since Elliot. Zane had only kissed me when he wanted sex, or when he wanted to persuade me to do something I didn't want to do, or when he wanted me to forgive him for something. But even then, his kisses weren't like this. They weren't so deep and urgent.

Con's room was beautiful: luxurious, with a sofa and a four-poster bed. There was a little fridge full of chocolate and drinks and stuff. Con pulled out two mini bottles of champagne and popped them open. We drank and kissed more on the sofa.

'Look,' I said, pulling away for a moment. 'This is as far as it goes. I'm not ready to . . .'

I didn't need to spell it out. Con put his arms around me and said, 'Shhhh. You don't need to explain. We'll do whatever you want. Or don't want. Your pace, OK?'

He told me that he wanted to see me again. I explained how I was scared of Zane finding me. I couldn't go to Suze's – he'd immediately know to look for me there. I took the risk of turning on my phone again. I had forty-seven messages, all from Zane.

'I'm gonna have to go back,' I said in despair. 'I got nowhere else to go.'

Con put his hands on my shoulders. 'Do you *want* to go back?'

'No!'

'Then you need never see him again,' he said. 'You have a choice, Emma. Either you go and find this Zane guy and live the sort of life where you end up wandering the streets penniless and frightened with your heels in your hand, or you stay right here and let me look after you.'

I stared at him. He was so kind. I couldn't believe my luck. 'OK. I'll stay with you, Con,' I said gratefully.

It was mad how quickly things had changed in one night.

TWENTY-SIX

Early the next morning, I rolled over and switched my phone back on. The minute I did, it rang.

It was Mum. She was frantic, crying, saying she'd been trying me all night. 'Are you with him, Emma? Are you with Zane? Are you at his flat?'

I sat up. I was still with Con in the hotel room. 'No, Mum, I'm not,' I said nervously.

'Oh, thank god. Don't go to his place, don't let him near you.'

'What's happened?' I asked, my heart pounding.

Zane had been round to the café, trying to find me. When Suze and my mum said I wasn't there, Suze had given him a piece of her mind – and Zane had *punched* her. And he hadn't gone round alone. Two men – from Mum's description, they could have been any of the guys from the club – were with him, and they'd smashed up the café too.

When Con woke up to see me sobbing and throwing on my clothes, he immediately asked me what was wrong. Then he insisted on coming to Suze's café with me. He got dressed, and called us a cab.

When we got there, I threw myself into my mum's arms.

'I'm so sorry, Mum, this is all my fault!'

Then I saw Suze, and sobbed even more. She had a cut on the side of her face, which was all bruised. She was holding some ice to her jaw with one hand and using the huge coffee machine to make herself some coffee with the other.

'Suze! I'm so sorry.' I was crying and crying. 'Here, let me do the coffee—'

'I can do it,' Suze snapped.

Mum looked at me and shook her head. I backed off. I didn't blame Suze for being angry with me. Con had found a dustpan and a bin bag, and helped Mum sweep the glass from where the men had smashed the stuff on the counter.

'Oh, your lovely café,' I said weakly. 'Suze, please, please talk to me. Are you OK? Are you sure that cut doesn't need stitches?'

'It's fine,' she sighed, not snapping this time. 'I know when a wound needs stitches and when it doesn't, trust me. I've seen it enough.'

She sipped her coffee, and I just stood there still crying and saying, 'I'm so, so sorry.'

'I warned you about him, didn't I?' Suze said, looking at me finally.

She *had* warned me. She'd had him worked out straight away, and I hadn't listened. And now she was injured, and her café trashed.

A fat tear rolled down her cheek. Suze *never* cried. She wiped the tear with the back of her hand and rubbed the small wet patch against her blouse.

Con had stayed quiet as he cleared up, probably not knowing what he'd walked into. Now he spoke. 'It's none of my business, but have you called the police?' he said. 'Would you like me to? Oh, I'm Con, by the way.'

Suze shook her head. 'There's no point, my love. We don't know who he knows. Best leave it.'

After we'd cleaned up the bulk of it, Con and I went upstairs. I went into Mum's room and changed out of that stupid red dress and the heels. Mum was only a bit bigger than me, so I found leggings and a T-shirt and some old trainers to wear.

'God, you look even sexier in those old clothes,' Con said when I came out of the bathroom. Then he sat me down and looked very serious. Serious and older all of a sudden. 'Emma, I want to help you' he said. 'And I want to help your mother. It's clear you're all in a fair bit of trouble here.'

'More like a total mess, but yeah,' I said, sniffing.

'Quite,' he agreed. 'Now, I have a flat, near my family home in London, that's suitable for you and your mother. These guys lured you into some seedy world because you're young and you have ambition, not to mention a ridiculous amount of beauty and charisma. Stay away for a bit, and when these goons are well and truly out of your life, I can get some decent marketing people to properly promote your brand.'

'But what if Zane finds us?' I asked, almost starting to cry again.

'Leave him to me,' said Con grimly. 'He won't bother you again. Guys like him just care about money. It will be taken care of.'

I stared, my jaw almost hanging open. Then I flung my arms round him. 'Con, I don't know what to say.' I wept into his shoulder. 'Would you really do this for me? I can't believe it. I'm so lucky I met you!'

He held me for a moment then gently pushed me back. 'This arrangement must be good for both of us. I want to spend time with you. If you're happy, I'm happy. OK?'

I nodded and said, 'OK . . .'

Mum was over the moon when I told her about Con's plan. Even Suze, normally suspicious, agreed that it sounded like a good idea. Perhaps it was the hit on the head.

Con did everything for us. He got a driver to come and help us move our things. I couldn't get my stuff from

Zane's, of course, but Con gave me money to buy more clothes and to get some bits and bobs for the flat, make it more personal.

The flat was a lovely little place. Much bigger than Nan's, and so near Kings Road, where all the really posh shops were. Mum was thrilled.

In the next couple of weeks, we managed to settle in. It certainly wasn't a chore. Mum still kept on one of her cleaning jobs, but she was more relaxed now. She walked around the flat as if she owned it. I was mostly with Con, of course. He'd come and pick me up and we went to parties and clubs and stuff, but nothing like I'd been doing with Zane. Much classier and friendlier. Sometimes he had parties at his own place, which was huge and absolutely gorgeous, and just around the corner from the flat.

'I want you to make each and every person feel welcome and looked after, OK?' he told me the first time he had a party. 'You're the hostess, remember that.'

The parties were boisterous and loud, full of his rich friends and people he'd worked with in places like Hong Kong and the Philippines. They were different to the people I'd met with Zane. I learned to talk to them on their wavelength, to play the part of hostess. I think my acting experience helped a lot.

'The fact that you haven't spent a gap year digging a well in Africa probably makes you the most interesting person in the room,' Con said to me. 'You're a real person leading a real life with challenges none of my friends have a clue about. I'm proud of you.' My confidence soared.

It wasn't too long before we started sleeping together. I'd go round to his, or if Mum was off out, he'd come round to the flat. Con was very loving in the bedroom. He wanted lots of cuddles and to be held afterwards. Nothing like Zane.

The bed in his place was huge, with black satin sheets, and there was a mirrored ceiling. 'This is so cheesy, I love it!' I told him the first time I saw it.

'The mirror was put up as a bit of a joke, so I could say to my old man "you did say I can decorate to my own tastes",' Con said. 'And it *was* funny. Mum wasn't too pleased, but Pops thought it was a hoot. Turns out though . . .' He came up behind me, put his arms around me and whispered in my ear, 'It really *is* a lot of fun.'

I turned around and kissed him.

Con was a banker in the city, but it was pretty clear he didn't really need to work. He had a large allowance from his family. The job thing was just to not look like a spoilt rich boy, I think. It was pretty clear that, to a lot of the girls Con knew, he was a good catch, so I had to be on the ball. I thought the Charlottes at school were posh, but these Esmes and Imogens were on another level. I had to concentrate on being the funny, sexy girl Con loved.

'So do you ski, Emma?' one of those girls asked me at a party in front of everyone, like it wasn't obvious I didn't come from the sort of family who went skiing.

'Do I ski?' I said, looking up and pretending to think. 'Does sliding down the slope by the Westfield car park on a bit of cardboard count? In that case, yeah! I'm an experienced skier.'

Con and his friends laughed. The girl pretended to find it funny too, but I knew she was frustrated that her put-down hadn't worked. After parties like that, I'd do impressions for Con and he'd have to guess which friend I was doing. I lounged back on the sofa, one leg casually on my knee. 'I was *meant* to be in Esfahan this evening, but the bloody Iranian government wouldn't give me a visa!'

'Ha!' laughed Con. 'That's Rupert, that's definitely Rupert. He's always banging on about Iran.'

I chuckled and nodded, then did another. 'Oh Emma, I *love* the way you talk, it's so refreshing! Isn't it *refreshing*, Con? It's so honest. Some of my ancestors were working class you know, so it's really lovely to connect.'

He hooted. 'Immie! God, she has no self-awareness. You do her voice perfectly!'

I grinned. 'You know this is always my favourite part of a party,' I told him. 'Sitting here with you and laughing about everything that happened. You're like a mate.'

'A mate that can't keep his hands off you,' Con said, kissing my neck. 'You know all my friends fancy the pants off you?'

I had clocked that. 'Do you get jealous?' I teased him.

'When I see you flirting madly? Making every man in the room lust after you? Yes, I get mad with jealousy. But also, it turns me on, because I know they'll be going home alone or with much less interesting women, and I'll get to sit with you at the end of the night demanding that you kiss me.'

We never made it off the sofa and into the bedroom on a lot of those nights, and I was actually happy.

*

I loved being with Con, but when he was at work, I wanted something to do. It was strange not even having the photo shoots to go to, and obviously school was off for the summer while we waited for our GCSE results. I messaged occasionally with Matilda and Soreya, but it was awkward. I felt worlds apart from them. I missed the rush of seeing my likes and followers going up on Insta, and the free stuff.

The @KissingEmma69 account had been taken down – not that I'd had much control over it anyway. I had a feeling they'd probably found another girl to build up into a sexy influencer. I also worried about whether they were still putting up my nude pics on that JustFans page.

'It drives me mad, Con!' I whined. 'I had almost forty thousand followers. How am I going to be an influencer rolling in cash from endorsements if I have to start all over again?'

Con said, 'I love your ambition, my little Elon Musk. You *will* rule the world eventually, you just have to be a bit patient. We'll build a much better account for you. You'll soon be fighting them off.'

I wasn't quite sure how he thought this could happen at first. But the more I thought about it, and saw what other girls were doing, the more I realised I could control the way I came across on my socials. Be more myself.

I remembered one of Con's mates from a party a couple of weeks ago had said that his job was something to do with social media branding. I asked Con about him.

'My mate Pierre? Yes, he's a wizard at that stuff – *and* he's obsessed with you.'

'He was the one that looks like a horse trapped in a lift door, right? Do you reckon he'd help me out?'

'That's the one,' said Con, chuckling. 'And yes, of course. He'd do anything for you.'

So Con arranged for us to go to dinner with Pierre.

'Your unique selling point,' Pierre told me, 'is that you're utterly, naturally beautiful. Old school Hollywood, almost.'

I liked the sound of that, especially the Hollywood part. That sounded more like what I was into. 'Like a classic actress type of vibe?'

'Yes! Exactly. Perhaps with minimal make-up, not like a typical influencer. You're bringing naked back.'

I pursed my lips. 'Been there, done that.'

'A naked *face*, I mean,' he said with a laugh. 'It will be totally different to your previous account.'

That definitely sounded good. I could do things differently, be something better. It was time to be more myself.

'Let's call it @therealEmmaHamilton,' I said.

So Pierre became my artistic director. I showed him a photographer I'd found while I was scrolling, called Senai Peters, and he got in touch with her. 'She's perfect,' he said. 'She's just starting to build her portfolio, so she'll work with us for next to nothing.'

Her photos were incredible – really arty close-ups of faces full of character and in exotic places like sand dunes. 'The ones she's taken of these girls in the desert are amazing!' I said. 'That shoot must have cost a fortune, though.'

'Those?' Pierre said, looking at my phone. 'Those sand dunes are in Rye, Sussex. Shows how talented she is if you thought it was the Sahara!'

The next weekend, Con drove me, Pierre and Senai to Brighton. It was super early in the morning so there weren't too many people on the beach yet. Senai was a tiny woman with dark hair chopped really short, and enormous dark eyes. She seemed really excited and danced about like a kid.

'You're so beautiful,' she said, snapping away, taking warm-up pictures as I stretched and smiled on the pebbles. This felt familiar, but also much more relaxed than with Zane and Joe.

'OK,' Pierre said. 'So we are going to stay true to looking natural and minimal. Face, hair, body, everything. Right?'

I nodded. I'd deliberately worn quite simple clothes – a strappy vest and denim shorts, trying to channel Marilyn Monroe on her day off. I posed with one strap hanging off my bare shoulder and smouldered towards the camera.

'Not too sexy, yeah?' Con asked. I kissed him for being so sweet.

Senai said, 'This is going to be tasteful, Con. She's in my hands, the best hands.'

In the car back Senai showed me some of the shots.

'I love them!' I gasped.

They were beautiful. Prancing about and posing against the gorgeous early morning sky and the sea behind me. I looked happy.

I got my new Insta account @therealEmmaHamilton up and running, and Pierre advised me on the best of Senai's shots to use. We used all the hashtags: #naturalbeauty #bareface #nakedface #emmahamilton #englishrose. This time I had control of the account, though. I had the password, I had final say on the photos that went on there. It was my life, my account.

The Brighton shoot got a lot of likes. In the back of my mind I was worried that Zane or Joe might notice, but things were quiet on that front, thank god. Next, we went to Trafalgar Square early one morning. I'd bought a vintage-style one-piece swimsuit, and I jumped in the fountain and posed in it, giggling hysterically. Luckily it was a hot June day. We also did some shots where I was wearing a huge admiral's hat by Nelson's Column. That was risky because we had no permission, and I was half naked in the middle of London, but Senai was fast and even persuaded me to straddle one of the lions like a Hollywood vixen. I almost fell off as Pierre hoisted me up there, I was laughing so much.

'Who was Nelson anyway?' I asked as our laughter died down.

'Nelson?' said Con. 'A naval hero. He beat the French at the Battle of Trafalgar. Without Nelson there'd have been no British Empire.'

Senai raised an eyebrow. 'Now wouldn't that have been a shame?' she said sarcastically.

'Hmm,' I said. 'And this would just be called "Square" with that big column with no one at the top.'

'"Trafalgar" comes from the Arabic "Taraf Al-Gharb", or Way of the West,' Senai added.

I giggled. 'Bloody hell, I can tell you two never went to the school I did.'

'And here's another fascinating fact for you,' Pierre said. 'Nelson had a mistress called Emma Hamilton.'

I stared at him. 'No way! That's my name.'

'I know, dolly, that's why I'm telling you,' said Pierre cheerfully. 'Emma, Lady Hamilton, actually. It was a huge love story back in their day. She was famous for being completely gorgeous. There are loads of paintings of her. Look her up.'

Early on, Con had got me a new phone to stop Zane from ringing me or trying to find me. I looked her up straight away. 'God, she was beautiful. Lady Hamilton,' I breathed. 'Why didn't Nelson marry her? Why was she just a mistress?'

'He was already married,' Pierre explained. 'It was a huge scandal. She was poor, and rich men fell in love with her but then went off and married women with money and titles. Emma was treated like a pet until they tired of her and passed her on. It was the only way for a girl like her to survive back in Georgian times. She was pretty much sent as a present to Lord Hamilton.'

'Well, *he* obviously married her,' I said, feeling suddenly protective of this woman who shared my name.

'He did, but he was so much older than her,' said Pierre. 'Still, she reinvented herself to fit into his world. Then she met Nelson and he truly fell in love with her. She was ambitious, like you.' It seemed we had hit on one of Pierre's favourite subjects. 'I was fascinated by their love story when I was reading History at university. That's why I was drawn to you, darling!' He tickled my ribs briefly, then sighed. 'Nelson died at Trafalgar and it broke Emma Hamilton's heart.'

'Poor Emma,' I said, looking at the picture on my phone.

'You know the worst thing?' said Pierre. 'When he was about to go into battle, he changed his will. He wanted Emma and the child they had together to be given money, looked after. But his wishes were ignored.'

I was horrified. 'Oh my god! Why?'

Pierre shrugged. 'Because she was common. Because it was such a scandal. Britain wanted Nelson to be remembered for his heroic deeds at sea, not for his affair.'

'So what happened to her?'

'She got into massive debt, went to prison, then fled to Calais, France.'

'I know where Calais is,' I said, rolling my eyes. 'I'm not a total doughnut.'

'She died there, of alcoholism. A tough yet glorious life.'

I looked again at the picture of poor Lady Emma Hamilton. I hoped alcoholism and heartbreak weren't on my horizon. But the rest sounded about right.

*

As my new Instagram started to build momentum, I had to start blocking some of the pervier DMs. Then I took charge of negotiating with the accounts that wanted to send me free stuff. Clothes, jewellery, shoes . . . The more followers I got (I was almost at thirty thousand after only a month), the more stuff I got sent. And this time it was all off my own back.

I started making videos, talking about my life. Being really honest, about all the crazy stuff that had happened to me in my sixteen years on this planet. More views, more followers, more interest rolled in. I did some funny stuff, too. The videos I made that got the most likes were when I did impressions of famous people. Soap stars, reality TV stars. I worked out a few scenes or jokes, practised their voices, then just filmed myself. People really seemed to love it, calling me 'multitalented'. Pierre and Senai were busy with their own careers, but if I sent them a video that needed some tweaks, they'd edit it for me before I posted it. It started to feel like a proper job, like I was a proper influencer.

The one thing I wasn't allowed to do was post any pictures with Con.

'My family have some high-profile businesses, Em,' he told me. 'They're just keen we keep our private lives very private, to avoid getting tripped up with anything on socials.'

I didn't tell him that I'd searched his name online and found pictures of him with other girls in the past. He didn't seem all that private back then. But they were all a certain type of posh girl, so that might have had something to do with it.

Still, Con spent most of his spare time with me at the flat with Mum. He seemed to like hanging out there, and obviously Mum loved him. I tried to ignore the little trickles of irritation that he was still so edgy if I even suggested posting a picture of the two of us together.

Mum had stopped cleaning all together now that I was making more cash again from endorsements. She took charge of managing the clothes and things I was sent, making sure I knew what to post when and that sort of thing. Turns out her superpower was getting in touch with designers and asking them to send me clothes for free in return for posting pictures of myself in them.

I was so busy that summer I didn't even think about my GCSE results. So it was a surprise when I checked my email on my phone and saw that they were up. Con was snoring away beside me, having stayed the night before, and my mouth was sort of dry as I clicked in to see what I'd got. I'd passed English, Maths, French . . . and Drama! Somehow I'd pulled off an 'A' for that.

'Four is more than I ever passed, my darling. I think it's brilliant!' Mum said when I told her about it. She was actually really over the moon.

Con, however, seemed a bit less impressed. 'Well done, darling,' he said absently when I showed him my results. 'I sometimes forget you're only sweet sixteen . . .'

I was just glad that I'd managed to do so well in the

subject that meant the most to me. My fingers hovered over the screen, ready to message Matilda and Soreya to see how they'd done, but something stopped me. That was the only thing that gave me a bit of a sinking feeling.

I missed my mates.

TWENTY-SEVEN

I didn't worry too much at first when my period was late. It had happened before. I was a whole week late once. But this time, after a few more days, I started to worry. Really worry. My boobs ached. There was something weird going on with my body. I took a pregnancy test: negative. But after another week, still no period. I panicked.

The internet told me I could still be pregnant, that I needed to wait, that really early on it doesn't always show as positive. I took another test: still negative, but still no period. Why was my body doing this to me? I was careful with Con, most of the time. He didn't like condoms and I didn't like diseases, so we'd both got checked out, and we were both fine. After that we didn't use condoms, but we were careful. Well, careful-ish. There were one or two accidents, if I'm honest.

Oh god. I couldn't be pregnant. Jesus Christ.

I took a third test. Two lines.

My body was making a baby. This was not in my plan. What was I going to do?

I told Mum before I told Con.

'Oh my god, Emma!' Mum wasn't angry. If anything, she sounded excited. 'How did that happen?'

'Jesus, Mum! Do you need me to draw a diagram?'

'Oh shush. Well. Con's a lovely man, he'll look after you.'

'Who says I'm going to keep it?' I muttered. I was younger than Mum had been when she'd had me.

But Mum was right. Con never said it outright, but he loved me, surely? Why else had he helped me so much, looked after me? I'd wanted for absolutely nothing since the day I'd met him. This might actually be a good thing. Once I told him, he'd be even more into me. And I'd finally get to meet his parents.

I'd asked about meeting them before, but now it was even more important. I decided to test the waters first.

'Would your family like me?' I asked him a day or so after I'd found out about the baby. Mum was out at Suze's, and I'd cooked us dinner.

Con laughed. 'Like you? They'd adore you!'

This was it. My chance. 'Maybe we should have them round or something?' I said in a rush. 'So I could meet them . . .'

Con looked away. 'They travel so much. If they're not in Hong Kong on business, they're off skiing somewhere. They dash in and out of London all the time, so it's hard to catch them.'

His mum's face suddenly flashed up on his phone screen to FaceTime him. As usual, he got up and went into the other room. Thinking about it, I'd never heard him mention me in any of these calls, or what we'd been up to. Tiny alarm bells started to ring.

I had to do it. And I had to do it now.

'Con, I've got something to tell you,' I began carefully when he came back into the kitchen. He looked at me, his face intense. My tone had worried him, I could tell.

'I'm pregnant,' I said.

His face turned to stone. 'What?'

'I-I'm having a baby. I'm pregnant.'

He frowned. 'You're kidding?' He actually seemed angry.

'Con, it's OK, it'll be all right,' I began.

But any part of Con that had ever been sweet and kind and funny seemed to drain out of him entirely in that one moment. 'Fucking hell!' He stood up from the table, his chair scraping loudly against the fancy tiled floor. 'Fuck!' he said again. He turned his back to me, leaning on the sink, his head bowed.

I was starting to get scared. 'Con, please, it's OK. We'll be fine!'

He turned to me. '*We'll* be fine? What the fuck do you mean, *we'll* be fine? What fucking planet are you on? This is all just a bit of fun on the side, Emma, don't you get it? I'm not trying to have an heir with some girl off the street.' He bent down right into my face, hissing the last word at me.

I was in shock. I hadn't seen him like this before. *Not again*, I said to myself silently.

'Con, I'm sorry. Please don't be angry—'

'Do you know what you've done, you stupid fucking bitch?'

He stormed out of the flat and slammed the door, leaving me to sob uselessly. Was that what he really thought of me? Some girl off the street? Just a bit of *fun*?

I told Mum what happened when she came back. Typically, she defended him. Said it would have been a shock for him, that he'd come back when he'd cooled down.

'Give him a chance,' she told me.

I think she was just worried about the idea of me with a baby but not the rich man to support us. I suppose I was starting to think that myself.

Con's text came an hour later.

I've transferred money into your bank account for an abortion and rent deposit for a new flat. I want you and your mother out by this evening.

He didn't even bother to ring me. I showed Mum the text message.

'Call him,' Mum insisted. 'He can't do this to you!' *To us*, I reckon she meant.

'I'll call him once we've gone,' I spat. 'I don't want to stay here another second.'

I was sick of men like Con, like Zane; Mo, Elliot, all of them. What did I ever really get besides hurt?

Since that day in Trafalgar Square, I'd read loads about Emma Hamilton, Nelson's Emma. She'd had a baby with a rich bloke when she was my age. He hadn't wanted her after that. His mate, Lord Greville, became her boyfriend instead. Lord Greville made her send her baby away, to her relatives miles away. He didn't let her raise her own child. Well, this wasn't the eighteen hundreds any more. I had choices.

I found myself calmly typing back to him, **I don't want to get an abortion, Con. I'm keeping the money though, to buy things for the baby.**

A minute later, my phone was ringing.

'You can't do that!' Con shouted down the phone. 'It's my baby too, and I demand you get an abortion.'

I felt my anger rise. 'You don't get to tell me what to do with my own body,' I said, and I put down the phone.

Mum and I packed fast, stuffing bin bags and cases with our clothes. There was quite a bit more than we'd come with, what with the endorsement products, and the stuff Con had bought me.

'I'll call Suze,' Mum said. 'She'll come in a taxi to help.'

'Tell her I'll pay.'

Mum and I had been in this zone before. We didn't talk, we just packed, urgently wanting to get out of a place we'd called home but which now felt like it was filled with poison. A new start, yet again.

But I was amazed at how calm I was. How in control. This would be fine. We could do this. We could finally sort things out on our own.

On my own.

An hour later, we were loading Suze's taxi with our stuff. I was careful not to take a single thing of Con's. We were quiet in the car. I didn't know what Suze knew.

'Has my mum said, Suze?' I asked at last.

'That you're pregnant? Yes, my love,' she replied. 'It'll all be fine. Don't you worry. You've got us.'

*

'If it's a girl you should call it Matilda, no question. Actually – if it's a boy you should call it Matilda, too.'

Chocolate milkshake almost came out of my nose as I laughed at that. Me and Soreya and Matilda were in Iceshack. Somehow, in the two weeks since everything that had happened with Con, I'd got up the courage to reach out to them. It felt weird to catch up about what they'd been up to over their summer holidays when so much had happened to me. While they were getting ready to start college, I was growing an actual baby inside me. A month off my seventeenth birthday, and I'd lived more life than most people twice my age.

'So can we come with you to the hospital?' Soreya asked. 'I've always wanted to see a baby being born.'

'Ah Soreya!' Matilda shrieked. 'I'm trying to enjoy my strawberry sundae. I don't want to think of a baby coming out of Emma's foof.'

'Foof? Who calls it a foof?' I giggled, rubbing my belly. I wasn't showing yet, not at all, but I felt conscious of the baby being there. I'd been a bit scared to tell Soreya and Matilda about being pregnant, but both of them had been really supportive. I couldn't believe how much I'd missed them. 'Anyway, there's months and months to go before I'm due to push anything out of anywhere.'

I had my first doctor's appointment that coming Monday. Mum and I had just signed a lease on a new flat round the corner from Suze's. It was poky, especially compared to where we'd been living with Con, but with Mum going back to some cleaning jobs, plus me still actually making some decent cash through my Insta influencing, we could afford it.

'It's mad that you're going to be having a kid while me and Matilda are just doing our A-levels,' Soreya said with a smile, draining the last of her milkshake. 'You'll have to rebrand your Insta to a mummy-blogging thing. I reckon you'll smash that, though.'

I had been thinking about that a bit. She was right. Things would be different, that was for sure. But I was convinced everything was going to work out for the best.

TWENTY-EIGHT

I'd just waved bye to Soreya and Matilda as they got on the bus when I felt it. A massive twinge, right in the lowest part of my belly. My hand flew there instinctively. A second later I doubled over in pain. My mum was at a cleaning job across town, so the first person I thought to call was . . .

'Suze? Something's wrong,' I gasped.

I was only a couple of streets away from the café. Even as I explained where I was, I could hear the bell above the door jingle as she slammed it shut. 'Stay there, darling,' Suze ordered. 'I'm coming to find you.'

I slumped on to the bench at a nearby bus stop, staying on the line as I heard Suze panting down the phone that she'd be there in a minute. It felt like less than that before she was standing over me, still breathing hard.

In a flash, she had me up with one arm under my armpit, helping me back to hers. She murmured reassuringly at me, but I could feel something was wrong.

I rushed to the bathroom when we got to the café, and cried out at the bright flash of blood in my underwear.

'All right, love. It's all right,' Suze said softly.

I could barely hear her through my tears.

My *baby*.

*

'Here you go, love,' Mum said, handing me a cup of tea.

I sat up straighter in bed back at our flat and gave Mum a weak smile. She and Suze had tried to persuade me to go to the hospital, but there didn't seem to be much point. I knew what had happened.

The baby was gone.

Matilda and Soreya came round almost every day over the next few weeks, taking it in turns to cheer me up with tales of their first days at the college up the road from our old school, of the Charlottes and how they were struggling to realise they didn't rule the roost in the same way that they used to. It was nice to have some light-hearted stuff to focus on, because what had happened with the baby hit me much harder than I'd expected.

I managed to get myself out of bed at last, and met the girls for a coffee at the Bunny Café. It was weird being back there, with Mrs Jeenal bringing us our drinks and a home-baked biscuit each with a wink.

'So good to see you, sweetie,' she said to me as she set mine down.

'Yeah, it is,' Matilda said as Mrs Jeenal left. 'We never usually get the good biccies.'

Soreya cleared her throat as a gaggle of boys crowded through the door. 'Don't look, all right, but—'

I turned towards the door – of course I did. Elliot stood among a group who'd come in from the college. He caught my eye the minute I looked over, and then looked away. And the funny thing was, I felt absolutely nothing. It felt like decades since all that stuff had happened. I was a different person now.

*

I called up Pierre a couple of days later. He was relieved to hear from me.

'After I heard what happened with Con, I was livid,' he said. 'I don't speak to him any more, Emma, I want you to know that. And I wanted to give you a bit of space, you know? I see that the @therealEmmaHamilton account is still thriving.'

Even though I'd obviously not posted much recently, my earlier posts had built and built in likes. So had my follower count. There had been a wobble a few weeks earlier, when some of the nude posts from the JustFans account had leaked and circulated around the sleazier corners of the internet. It was pretty shit that Joe and Zane were still making money off me and my body, but what could I do? Nothing, other than just let it go. I felt different now, more in control.

I explained to Pierre that I wanted to do some more photos with him and Senai in the next few weeks and he sprang into action, saying he'd gladly arrange it.

When I got back to the flat, Mum was out at one of her cleaning jobs. Something told me now might be a good time to make a new video. I'd barely any make-up on, but the raw look suited my mood. I took a deep breath and hit record.

'Hey guys. It's been a while. I want to tell you a bit about what's been going on with me . . .'

It all came pouring out – all the way back to how things had been with Dad, the bullying, my disappointment with the nudes that had leaked, my pride in my body. I spoke about how I had been taken advantage of, though didn't dignify Zane and Joe by naming them. How I'd been taken advantage of by men like Con too, who thought they were good until it came to the crunch. I broke down in tears when I explained what had happened with the miscarriage. And by the time I'd finished, I felt like a massive burden had been lifted.

I was ready to start a new chapter.

*

I could barely keep up with the reaction to my video. My phone was pinging with so many notifications that I had to switch it off for a while. People were impressed by my honesty about being pregnant, especially as a younger woman, and how devastating losing the baby had been. The crowning moment was an email from *Ella* magazine, asking if I'd sit down for a full interview with them, photo shoot and everything. A glossy mag, just like the ones I used to stare at and dream of seeing myself in back in the day. It was actually going to happen.

'They want me to be a part of their "Everyday Feminists" issue!' I told Mum.

Mum shrieked with delight, and set about taking over to arrange it all. 'Let's say I'm your manager, eh? It's good enough for Kris Jenner . . .'

I laughed. I wasn't interested in being a Kardashian type. Not any more, anyway. Because being the real Emma Hamilton was starting to work out.

Among the emails flooding into my inbox, I noticed a familiar name: Mrs Delerosh. I opened my old drama teacher's email. She said how proud she had been at my GCSE result, and that she'd heard of a course that I might be a good fit for.

It speaks to all your particular talents as the wonderful actress you are. But places are limited – the course is very exclusive. I would be

**happy to endorse you for it, but let me know if
you would be interested . . .**

A full-on drama course, in North London. The minute I read it, I knew this was it. My next step, what I really wanted to do. I was finally making my own money with the influencing stuff, but this seemed like the perfect next step. *Actual acting.*

Mrs Delerosh had left a phone number at the bottom of her email. I rang it quickly, telling her that I'd love to do it, if there were still spaces on the course.

'Perfect!' she said.

I grinned into the phone. Yeah. It was.

EPILOGUE

'Are you nervous, darling?' Mum asked as I checked my reflection in the bathroom mirror and then snapped a quick selfie for Insta.

'Sort of,' I admitted as I came out of the bathroom.

Mum picked up the magazine off the bed, beaming. I couldn't help a grin too, as she flicked to the double-page spread again. 'How can you be nervous, eh?' she said with pride. 'You're *the* Emma Hamilton! If those drama snobs get up their own arses, just show them this!'

I shook my head and laughed. 'Thanks Mum.' Then I turned serious. I knew she was joking around, but it hit me just how far we had come, both of us. How I'd have been nowhere without her. How hard things had been for her, too. 'Really. Thank you.' And I hugged her tightly.

She squeezed me back. 'I know, love.'

One day past my seventeenth birthday and I had been through some tough stuff. But we had a flat at last. We weren't struggling for money any more like we used to. There were no more angry men in my life telling me what to do – not my dad, or Mo, or Elliot, or Zane, or Con, *none* of them.

I was single, and I had no plans to be anything other than that for a good long while. I was happy with myself, with the me that everyone was now getting the chance to know, online and in real life. The only time I planned to be someone else was on the stage or screen, learning a script. The first step towards that was today, on the first day of my course. This was something just for me.

As I glanced one last time at my reflection in the mirror by the door, I realised I was proud of myself. I was happy – and I deserved to be.

I smiled.

AUTHOR'S NOTE

At primary school, I learned all about Horatio Nelson –
England's great naval hero whose statue sits on, well, Nelson's
column in Trafalgar Square. The square was of course
named after the Battle of Trafalgar, which Nelson won but
also died at, in 1805. We performed a play about his life. It
was a musical extravaganza (I was the narrator, in case
you're wondering). One of the songs was about Emma, Lady
Hamilton (played by Tanya Forward in my class. I seethed
with envy, in case you're wondering), his mistress and the
love of his life. I was fascinated by her. When I was much
older, I found books about Emma which didn't simply dismiss
her as Nelson's bit on the side or just refer to her beauty.

She came from a very poor background, had no formal
education and was working as a maid when she was just
twelve. Like all women in that part of history, without a man
to look after her she would be destitute. Options were very

limited for women. Their choices were often to get married, be looked after by male relatives, be the mistress of a married man who could keep them, or be a servant or a sex worker.

Emma was horribly let down by many rich men who saw her as a beautiful ornament to be used, then cast aside when they'd had enough. But Emma reinvented herself and had a spectacular life outside the boundaries of her social class. She educated herself, used her artistic talents (she sang and danced and enthralled her audiences), intelligence and abundant humour to fit in with the highest echelons of society. She was fantastically famous in Georgian times as an artist's model and for being beautiful.

When she met Nelson, they fell madly in love and had a child. Just before he fought at Trafalgar, Nelson changed his will, asking his King and Country to look after Emma if he was killed. He was shot dead on board his ship, HMS Victory, and because his relationship with Emma was considered a scandal (he was still legally married to someone else) and because Emma was seen as a party girl of a lower social class, his wishes weren't honoured and Emma died alone, penniless and heartbroken. A rotten way to treat this phenomenal women, or any woman.

I'm outraged that to this day she is so often dismissed as merely the mistress of a powerful man. She was, in her way, thoroughly modern in her attitudes, believing her class should not hold her back, grabbing what happiness and success she could from life. I wanted to take a girl like Emma and place her in our modern day. I wanted to create my own Emma who has nothing but her own wits to live on. I wanted to explore how our society still judges women according to their looks, and how it is still so easy for young girls to fall into exploitative relationships. I wanted to give my Emma the choices and agency the real Emma Hamilton did not have. I wanted to write a story which paid tribute to women who refused to know their place.

ACKNOWLEDGEMENTS

My thanks first and foremost, as ever, to my children, Cass and Vivie for bringing such kindness, fun and humour to my life. You two were all I needed in lockdown.

Love and gratitude to Will, aka The Tall Man, who looked after them so much and so brilliantly while I wrote this. Thanks too to Sophie-from-down-the-road and Catherine-round-the-corner and Noreen-by-The-Plough for being such kind and supportive friends and for letting me throw my youngest child into their homes when I needed to. Thanks to Corry and Christian for all the overnights when I wanted to get away and write. Hali-over-the-road, thank you my friend, for all the chats, walks and coffees from your fancy machine. New friendships with fellow dogwalkers were a tonic in lockdown, when I was still finishing this book. Huge love to you all, especially Khalid and Poonam.

Thank you to all my pals in our lovely little corner of Ealing where we were locked together this past year.

Thank you to everyone at Hachette, Helen Thomas for asking me and Rachel Boden for being patient!

My thanks also to Sareeta Domingo and Halimah Manan for reading this and giving me their thoughts. Thanks to Alison Padley for the cover design and Fortuna Todisco for its illustration. My good friend Heathcliff O'Malley took my picture . . . thanks Heathcliff for doing it when I know you have much bigger pics to fry.

RESOURCES

Much of *Kissing Emma* is about the journey through recognising damaging relationships and surviving them. If you're struggling, know that you're not alone, and if you're in an abusive situation, know that it's not your fault, no matter what anyone tells you. The websites below can help.

Love Respect
Aimed at 16–25 year olds, exploring what is and isn't a healthy relationship – from physical violence to coercive control
loverespect.co.uk

The Cybersmile Foundation
Aimed at young people, this website offers advice on cyberbullying – from catfishing to embarrassing pictures or videos of you being put online, to direct abuse and harassment
cybersmile.org

Hot Peach Pages

An international directory of sexual and domestic violence agencies, giving information and support for every woman and girl on Earth

hotpeachpages.net/index.html

Southall Black Sisters

Help for Black (Asian and African-Caribbean) and minority ethnic women and children who have been victims of violence and abuse

0208 571 9595 southallblacksisters.org.uk

Men's Advice Line

A helpline for male victims of domestic abuse

0808 8010327 mensadviceline.org.uk

Miscarriage Association

A helpline for anyone who's experienced a miscarriage

01924 200799 miscarriageassociation.org.uk

Mermaids UK

Helping gender-diverse young people and their families

0808 801 0400 mermaidsuk.org.uk

BELLATRIX *[noun: female warrior]*

In literature and in life, women of the past and present
have a million stories that are untold, mis-told or unheard.

Bellatrix is a collection of gripping, powerful and diverse YA
novels by leading female voices. From gothic to thriller
to romance to funny, each book is entirely unique,
but linked by a passion for telling *her whole story*.

HER STORY
THE WHOLE STORY

BELLATRIXBOOKS.CO.UK
#BELLATRIXBOOKS